Additional praise for

A FAMILY MATTER

and

CLAIRE LYNCH

"A beautiful and tender exploration of parental love, prejudice, and the things we carry that we don't even fully understand; the terrible decisions made in ignorance, and the almost unbearable consequences."

—Rachel Joyce, author of *The Unlikely Pilgrimage of Harold Fry*

"Claire Lynch takes elements of shame and stigma in our recent history and turns them into fiction that is beautiful, moving, and challenging. Every page sings out with empathy and love, pain and honesty. This unputdownable book—so precise, so deceptively simple, so beautiful in its tiny moments—will change the way you look at the world."

—Emilie Pine, author of *Notes to Self*

"I was blown away by this book. To tackle heart-wrenching emotion with such precision and restraint takes one hell of a talent. *A Family Matter* is an impeccable debut that turns the mess of life into something beautiful. A timely reminder of love's redemptive power."

—Lotte Jeffs, author of *This Love*

"I'm full of admiration for this novel, which strikes the satisfying balance of being both quietly observed and deeply felt. It's an intimate portrait of expectation, love, and restraint written with great sensitivity and warmth. I adored it."

—Chloë Ashby, author of *Wet Paint*

A FAMILY MATTER

A Novel

CLAIRE LYNCH

SCRIBNER

New York   Amsterdam/Antwerp   London
Toronto   Sydney/Melbourne   New Delhi

Scribner
An Imprint of Simon & Schuster, LLC
1230 Avenue of the Americas
New York, NY 10020

To all those who try their best.
That is all you can ever do.

why shouldn't
something
I have always
known be the
very best there is. I love
you from my
childhood,
starting back
there when
one day was
just like the
rest, random
growth and
breezes, constant
love, a sand-
wich in the
middle of
day

FROM EILEEN MYLES, "PEANUT BUTTER," 1991

I've walked there picking mushrooms at the edge of
    dread, but don't be fooled
this isn't a Russian poem, this is not somewhere else
    but here,
our country moving closer to its own truth and dread,
its own ways of making people disappear.

FROM ADRIENNE RICH, "WHAT KIND OF TIMES ARE THESE," 1995

JULY 2022

An unexpected item

Five and a half hours after he found out he was dying, Heron drove to his favorite supermarket. In the absence of an alternative, and because it was a Thursday, he decided to stick to his routine.

It is no secret that Heron likes to do his weekly food shop on a Thursday. In the evening, if at all possible, late afternoon at the earliest. His family teases him about it, his strange inflexibilities.

"Live a little," his daughter had said last week. "Go shopping on a Monday morning, I dare you."

But Thursdays are quiet and that suits him. Thursdays are sensible. Heron likes to start the weekend with a full fridge, although his weekends are, in truth, much like any other day of the week now.

At the top of the escalator he finds a small shopping cart; a perfect compromise, he has always thought, since a big cart is really too much, a basket not quite enough. Heron is an organized shopper, placing each item into the reusable bag he has labeled for its corresponding kitchen cupboard. He keeps the cleaning products separate from the bread. He doesn't rush, or forget the milk, or squash the salad. Heron isn't one of those people who minds when they change the layout of the supermarket from time to time. If anything, he sort of enjoys it, the hint of scavenger hunt it gives to tracking down the thin-cut marmalade. He could not say, if asked, why he shops in this particular way, the system speaks for itself.

Heron pushes his small cart to the farthest, coldest corner of the supermarket. For obvious reasons, frozen foods are always selected last. Today, in a significant break from routine, he slides open the glass lid of a waist-high chest freezer, flattens out the bags of potato smiley faces, and climbs inside.

It is the smell rather than the cold he notices first. Even with the lid slightly open, the air inside the freezer is stale and starchy. He is as surprised as anyone to find it is actually quite comfortable inside a chest freezer, even with the frost starting to soak through at the backs of his knees. Heron adjusts his shoulder blades, stretches out his legs, and the frozen potato faces settle beneath him. He lies still in the muffled peace of the chest freezer, and he lives.

Heron had felt sorry for the doctor in a way, a youngish woman, fiddling with her pen despite her best intentions. It can't be easy to have to say it out loud to someone.

"There are leaflets. And websites," the doctor had said, and then she moved, just slightly, reaching out to touch her desk to show him that this part, at least, was over. Heron had stood up too fast, tangling his jacket on the back of the chair, saying, absurdly, "It's showerproof."

And still, it wasn't as cold as you would think, in the freezer, or maybe it was so cold he couldn't tell anymore; that was a thought.

Heron looks up through the fog on the glass lid. He looks beyond, to the fluorescent lights and steel joists of the supermarket ceiling.

There are things he will have to do now. Things he will have to say. Admit.

He looks at the ice dripping and shining on the inside walls of the freezer beside his head. The manic smiles and hollow eyes of the potato faces. He looks at these things and he is fine. Heron is so fine that he might have simply stayed in the freezer forever, had a woman not slid open his lid in search of frozen petits pois and screamed.

It takes three members of staff to get him out. He is, as it turns out, quite cold indeed. The back of his head wet, his knees sore and stiffened. The manager is very good about it, cheerful even, when he says, "Let's get you out of there, sir, shall we?" and, "Is there someone we can call?"

It is only when he gets home that Heron understands the tone of the manager's voice. Calm, tolerant, as if a man reclining in a freezer was just something one expects in a varied retail career. Heron understands then what the manager saw. A confused old man. Not quite all there. Not quite all here.

Local news

Before bed, Heron calls his daughter on the landline. He doesn't like to use his mobile in the house. "Just me," he says, as he always does. Then he pauses, waits for her to say, "Hello stranger," or "Long time no hear," as she does, without fail, every night.

When Maggie asks Heron about his day, he has plenty to say. He tells her about the young couple across the street, laying a new lawn, as if they haven't even noticed the hosepipe ban. He tells her, in quite some detail, about an interesting radio documentary on wind farms. Had she caught it?

She hadn't.

Heron talks and Maggie makes the sounds of listening.

Uh-hmm. Yup. "Interesting," she says, or "Lovely."

Heron talks, but some things don't come up. The hospital, for example. The supermarket. Some things are best papered over, Heron thinks. For now. All of that would come out the wrong way if he tried to explain it. Instead, he sticks to safer topics: the new seed catalog that arrived yesterday. The free coffee waiting for him on his loyalty card. Maggie listens, and she waits for a gap, the chance to escape the conversation with, "Well, I'd better let you go. Sleep well."

Heron lets her take it, a way out for both of them.

"You too."

"'Night, then. Goodnight."

"Let's hear it," Conor says. "What's the latest press release from the neighbor's loft conversion?"

"Nothing to report," Maggie tells her husband. "It's a slow news day."

She pours two glasses of wine, fridge-cold and slightly too full for a Thursday evening. As she hands one to Conor, she can see he's a bit disappointed. Heron's nightly phone calls are usually a rich seam. She'd heard Conor at a party once, joking with their friends that he knew more about his father-in-law's greenfly problem than he did about politics in the Middle East. She knew she was supposed to laugh along, see the funny side of Heron's strangeness. But Maggie hadn't found it funny. She didn't mind that her dad told her everything; it had always been like that. All the little details of his day, his current thoughts and theories. Conor couldn't understand it, or wouldn't. Instead of laughing, Maggie had said in front of everyone, "Maybe you should try reading the newspapers a bit more carefully, darling," and they had driven home from the party in silence.

Glasses empty, they lock up the house, feed the cat. Conor gathers up his laptop and charger for work in the morning, saving time. Maggie checks the schedule on the fridge, all the things the children will need tomorrow. Tom's hockey stick, the packed lunches, a form Olivia needs Maggie to sign for the school camping trip. There are different things for the next day and the day after that. It is her job to remember the things, even though the children aren't babies anymore, even though Conor is a grown man quite capable of managing harder tasks than reading the carpool rota for himself. Still, she will do it, keep them all moving forward. Keep them all on track.

JULY 1982

A jumble

On the front steps of the church hall, two teenage girls shake a plastic bucket of change, making the coins jump and ring.

"Twenty pence to come in. Ten for children," they shout on singsong repeat.

Dawn checks her purse. It's early in the month, so she's fine, but she needs to make it last. A new salon has opened on the high street and the apprentices will give you a cut and blow-dry for free if you come in after hours. If she does that, she can put her haircut money toward the denim jacket she's seen in the catalog.

She can see that the proceeds from the jumble sale are going toward something or other. The church roof? The lepers? She can't read the label taped onto the bucket, the carefully felt-tipped bubble writing. "It's for us!" the Girl Guides say when they see her squinting to read it. "We need a new camping stove."

Dawn recognizes one of the girls; she went to school with her older sister, a lifetime ago, five minutes ago. She drops her coins into the bucket and the girls smile their matching metal smiles back at her.

When she was little, Dawn's nan took her to jumble sales near the posh houses on the weekends. Dawn liked to buy one thing to wear and one thing she could hold in her hand. On a good day the contents of her beaded purse would stretch to both. A new skirt and a bangle, say, or, on one memorable occasion, an almost new PVC raincoat and a key ring of the Eiffel Tower. On the bus journeys home, her nan would gossip with women who still wore hatpins, and Dawn would pray that nobody at school would recognize her new favorite top as their own castoff. Dawn still liked the bus ride across town, and she still had a taste for fashion that didn't match her budget. She came to the jumble sales on her own now, searching for treasure under the piles of discarded slacks, the outgrown school uniforms.

Everybody knew that the best clothes would go first. Older women pulling tartan trolleys outmaneuvered young women leaning on prams. All of them experts, selecting or discarding, checking labels in search of St. Michael, the patron saint of sturdy seams. Dawn works her way around the hall, smooth and smiling as a politician, never turning up her nose at a stained blouse, just in case its former owner turns out to be the woman on the other side of the trestle table. She runs her hand over some children's clothes, a pair of worn-in jeans, a mustard-yellow jacket with Rupert the Bear embroidered on the chest pocket. She keeps close to the tables, reaching out to touch sleeves and hems, the fabrics and patterns of other people's memories.

Halfway round the hall Dawn finds it, the perfect thing she didn't know she was looking for. From underneath a pile of crocheted baby blankets, she pulls out an Aran cardigan in wool the color of fresh cream. The last thing anyone else would want to buy in July. As she holds it up against herself for size, the woman across the table says, "Seventy-five pence." Then, laughing, "I'd say a pound, but God knows what'll happen when you try and wash it." Dawn thanks her, drops her coins in the ice cream tub, and takes one last look around to check nothing has been overlooked. The table of bric-a-brac is more than she can face today, as are the shoes, shaped by other people's feet, bound in their pairs by rubber bands.

Nobody is expecting her home for at least an hour, so Dawn finds the refreshments table and splurges on a cup of tea and a butterfly cake. Across the hall, a pair of elderly women are appraising some flesh-colored support garments, and Dawn watches as they tug from opposite sides, checking whether or not they'd be up to another deployment.

"Carnaby Street, eat your heart out," says the woman at the next table, and Dawn splutters a mouthful of tea back into her cup. She looks up to see a young woman scraping her chair over to the table, setting her blue cup and saucer right beside Dawn's. She leans toward her, smiles at her as if they weren't complete strangers.

"Any good finds?"

And that is it, they are talking.

They talk about the things they didn't buy, the things they did. Dawn fishes the cardigan from her shopping bag and holds it up for inspection. The buttons are like horse chestnuts, Dawn thinks, that is what it is.

"Hand-knitted." The woman nods her approval. "Must have taken hours."

"That's what I thought too. She gave it to me for less than a quid. You?"

The woman reaches into the wicker basket at her feet and begins to unwrap one of the newspaper packages. Dawn takes the chance to look at her, to work her out. They are the same age, or thereabouts. She seems tall, although it's hard to tell when she's sitting down. A bit posh, Dawn thinks, from the way she speaks. From the way she takes it for granted that Dawn wants to talk to her. Dawn wants to ask her where her earrings are from. The package unwrapped, crumpled newspaper spread across her lap, the woman holds out a champagne coupe from a set of four, small and shallow with a delicate green stem. The women look at the glass together, the light catching it. A beautiful but impractical thing.

"For all the dinner parties I never have," she says. "Chin-chin!"

She raises the empty glass with a flourish, her voice a little too loud for a person sitting in the refreshment corner of a church jumble sale, and sets the Mother's Union committee tutting. The woman grins and Dawn blushes, hot to her hairline, as people turn to look. Dawn had come here for a break, the chance to hide in an old version of herself for a couple of hours. It is a surprise that the morning has become a tiny adventure. When the woman catches her eye, Dawn feels she is an accomplice, caught, as she always had been at school, in the company of someone bolder, on the edge of fun that wasn't quite hers. The woman hadn't minded making a scene at all, she simply rewrapped the glass in its newspaper, placed her empty teacup carefully back on its saucer, and said, "I think I'll head off."

And Dawn, to her immense surprise, heard herself say, "Me too."

It was nothing, what happened next, the two of them bursting through the swing doors of the church hall like they were fleeing the scene of a bank raid. Hazel, becoming Hazel to her, introducing herself.

"Named for the color of my hair, apparently. Or was it my eyes? Who knows. My brother always said it was because they could tell I'd be nuts."

Her pretend sulk when Dawn had laughed and said, "No, I get it. I mean, I've only known you five minutes, but I see his point."

It was the best kind of summer Saturday. Cut grass everywhere and somebody lighting up a barbecue. Hazel, chatting, unstoppable, telling Dawn that she'd just moved to town, a little flat right beside the school so she'd be ready for the start of term.

"It's only my second job since training college. The kids are going to eat me alive," she said, hoping it was a joke. Dawn, who had lived in the village all her life, tried to impress when Hazel quizzed her about the local pubs, or what there was to do in this place that seemed to be just fields and houses. Houses and fields. When she thinks of it in bed that night, Dawn squeezes her eyes shut with embarrassment, pictures herself telling Hazel with such country-mouse certainty that the Horse and Groom was better than the Plough. Cringes at the way she'd gone on about the chips being tastier at the Princes Fish Bar, even though it was a shorter walk to Captain's Chippy. She remembers how Hazel had laughed and said, "Just the insider information I was hoping for," and Dawn had blushed again, trying desperately to muster up something more appealing to say about her hometown.

"The trains to London are regular," she had offered, finally, which just made Hazel laugh even more.

When they arrived outside Dawn's house, she had nodded at it, at its pebbledash and hanging baskets, and said only, "This is me."

Hazel had smiled, told her how great it had been to chat with someone who wasn't a hundred years old, or seven. And then she had waved at Dawn, huge enthusiastic waves, as if she were heading off on a long sea voyage, not just walking down the concrete path to her front door.

She knew she should have mentioned them, the husband and child waiting inside, her real life. It wasn't a lie, Dawn told herself, just a break, a few hours of being a different kind of young again. Not caring about anything except shopping and new friends and talking. She would tell Hazel the next time, if she even saw her again. Dawn had closed the door behind her that day and imagined Hazel walking away, down the dip of the hill into the center of the village, past the second-best pub and the bus shelter. She imagined her walking along the last little streets and up the stairs to her flat beside the school gates. Then she filled the kitchen sink with cold water and put her new-old cardigan in to soak.

AUGUST 2022

On rest

Maggie holds her phone above her head and snaps a photo of the sky, picture-perfect blue, to prove it or record it. For a few seconds she looks at the blue square, then she presses delete. She is pleased with her luck, finding a spot on this bench, warm in the lunchtime sun. It is one of those modern designs, divided by armrests, to save people from the awkwardness of touching elbows with a stranger. To deny the homeless the relative dignity of sleeping on a bench. She eats and she watches people dashing across the square with salads and green juices or taking phone calls with the thin air. She is surrounded by people with unseen purpose, their walking almost a jog, a little skip and hop of self-important busyness. Taking a proper lunch break is her boss's idea. "For balance," she had said, and more nauseatingly, "Rest is self-care, Maggie." As if sitting on a bench eating a Pret sandwich was indistinguishable from a weeklong Nordic spa break. Maggie is skeptical on the topic of rest. She suspects it is a waste, perhaps even a weakness. She is prone to thoughts like this lately, about time passing too quickly, or running out altogether. About everything slipping out of her grasp. When she told Conor she felt this way, he said it was just her age, textbook midlife crisis. Maggie had advised him, on the grounds of his own health and safety, not to offer that as an explanation again. She takes another picture of the blue sky and posts it online.

Maggie had argued that morning with her son, the usual battle over what kind and how much food made for a suitable breakfast. Then something about people taking too long, or not long enough, in the shower. And it was fine. Just family life, bustling and real. Except sometimes, when it was lonely. Tom made fun of her, she knew that, and lately he patronized her, too. Maggie thought it was probably inevitable, a necessary pulling away. But this morning she saw it more clearly, observed them all as a visitor might. She has made her son all those admirable things—confident, tall—and now she has to live with him walking around her house, full of the knowledge that other lives are already calling to him. At fourteen, Tom can almost see it, a life that is bigger, or sharper, than his parents'. A life not lived around bean-to-cup coffee machines and mindful lunch breaks. And Maggie knows she makes it worse, not better, filling the air between them with all the boring things mothers say, about working hard at school and good things coming to those who wait. She keeps talking to him, even when he says the color of her favorite coat reminds him of cat food, or that the TV programs she likes to watch are "bourgeois." Sometimes she laughs it off. Teenagers. Sometimes she is simply too tired to argue with him, so she disappears into the screen of her laptop, pretending to work, while searching for a gadget that might unblock the sink. Or buying a new dress that will take her from day to night, whatever that means. Any task that lets her hide in plain sight. Because sometimes he is right. Sometimes Maggie has to fight the urge to say to this boy who knows next to nothing, yes, fine. You have a point. I agree, actually. There ought to be more to life than washing machines and emails and remembering to put out the recycling on the right day. But life is also this. It is all of this.

The importance of a strong core

Heron takes the tablets the doctor gives him, and the tablets make him fat. To manage this side effect, the doctor tells Heron to walk, so he walks. Some days, he walks laps around the town center, adding on small errands to give his day a sense of purpose. On others, he crusts his walking boots with mud, walking the tractor-ridged paths in the fields behind his house. On the days he doesn't feel like walking, Heron lifts heavy things in the garden. He puts them down. He lifts them again. Both the walking and the tablets make him tired, but he must keep moving. He needs to build strength, not lose it, the doctor says. He must press on. At the end of the summer the doctor asks Heron if he has ever considered joining the gym.

Maggie has noticed the weight but not mentioned it; she wouldn't dream of it. It is just a part of getting older, she tells herself. When Heron announces he's bought a pair of trainers, she's as surprised as the rest of them. Just the idea of Heron on a running machine is hilarious to his family. There are several jokes about Lycra, and when his son-in-law calls him "Mr. Motivator," the children have to google the name and the results leave them in a state for the rest of the afternoon. Heron ignores them. He tolerates it. He should have joined years ago, he says.

Each week Heron meets Jacob, as arranged, at the exercise bikes next to the water cooler. Jacob is a personal trainer, prescribed by the hospital, no less. He is young and very keen on Heron engaging his core. Jacob's gym shoes look brand-new, and when Heron asks him about it, he explains that he keeps a special pair for work in his locker and never wears them outside. Heron likes Jacob; he likes the little sheets of paper he gives him to tick off his reps and sets; he likes all the new things he teaches him about protein shakes. Heron is not the oldest here, not by a long way. His family have got it all wrong. The gym is full of people in their long-loved bodies, preserving them, strengthening them, doing their part. Still, it isn't easy. Heron's body has forgotten how to move like this, or never knew. He nods as Jacob teaches him how to lunge.

"Back straight," he says. "A bit lower if you can."

Heron does as he is told, or does the best he can. He wonders if he could explain to Jacob how disorientating it is, the way a body changes. He hadn't even noticed it happening really; he just caught his reflection in the bathroom mirror one morning and saw it was his father's. It will happen to Jacob too, Heron thinks, though he won't tell him that. Gray chest hair, aches in the shoulders and hips.

On his way home from the gym, Heron pops into the corner shop to buy some bleach, lemon-scented, since they have it. Other responses to cancer were available, he knew that, but the kitchen floor was long overdue, and the doctor did say to carry on as normal. After his divorce, Heron was careful never to let standards slip around the house. He'd seen it happen often enough, men who ought to know better, living in bedsits, the smell of damp clothes all through the place, and crumbs in the stair carpet. Heron thought it was a shame to see men with estate cars and pensions who couldn't clean a toilet. If anything, divorce had given Heron the opportunity to fully embrace his domestic side. In the week after his wife left, Heron drew up his first schedule for cleaning the house. Hoovering upstairs one week, downstairs the next. Dusting every Sunday night. In the second week, he taped an inventory to the freezer door so he could maintain oversight of the contents, ticking chicken Kievs and choc ices off the list as he ate them. Heron actually liked to keep the dishcloth rinsed and neatly folded over the tap to dry. He kept a pen and notebook beside the phone, the spare keys under a tomato plant in the greenhouse. Single life wasn't a shock to him in the way it is for some men. It suited him; everyone said so. Especially the women who popped in with this or that excuse. Dropping Maggie off from dance class, or finding some other compelling reason to set foot in the house for a look around. Many a husband might take a leaf out of his book, they'd say, learn to take the mop out for a quick spin across the kitchen tiles. And Heron would smile, bat it all away, the model divorcé.

"It's nothing remarkable," he would insist; he was just doing what he needed to do to keep the house tidy for Maggie, now it was just the two of them. Besides, he liked to joke, it was all his dusting that made his wife leave him in the first place.

AUGUST 1982

Good fences

After the jumble sale, Dawn saw her everywhere. She saw the back of Hazel's head as she stood, four people back, in the queue at the newsagent's and had to hide behind the penny sweets until she left, rather than face the prospect of simply saying hello. Later that same week, Dawn saw Hazel waiting for a bus into town, an empty string bag over her arm. There were hints of her when she cut through the park on her way home. Shadows and suggestions of Hazel everywhere Dawn went. There were glimpses of Hazel behind her eyelids when she blinked. Dawn wasn't looking for her any of those times, but she saw her anyway. It was her haircut, bobbed to the jawline, the fringe a perfect straight line as if made with a spirit level and ruler. Dawn saw Hazel everywhere because she really admired her haircut.

One Tuesday evening, Dawn opened the front door to put out the empty milk bottles and saw Hazel, inexplicably there, at the end of the path. A coincidence, Hazel claimed, her evening walk just happening to bring her past at that exact moment. The coincidence happened again on Wednesday, and on Thursday. Then it kept happening. Dawn, an empty milk bottle in each hand; Hazel, leaning on the front gate, chatty, ready to listen. Dawn, talking about herself, drop by drop. Heron's job, his grand plans for the garden. Something funny their little girl had said at breakfast time, asking if dogs were boys and cats were girls. Hazel, offering up her failed efforts to make her flat seem more stylish with macramé plant holders. All the low-level madness she'd overheard in the post office queue that week. Tiny stories from their day that added up to something. A way of getting to know each other. Dawn would laugh until her cheeks ached. Then hurry back inside the house to her real life. Sometimes she would catch sight of herself in the hall mirror, see the flush across her face, the muddle she was getting herself in over a doorstop chat. Dawn couldn't under-stand it, the way Hazel made her nervous. The feeling that her mouth was full of all the things she would say if she wasn't too embarrassed to put herself into words.

Then one evening, speaking across the front gate, Hazel sug-gests a shandy, "as the weather is so warm. The Horse and Groom, obviously."

Dawn runs back inside to grab her handbag. She won't be late, she calls out, she has her keys. It's as good as Maggie's bedtime anyway. They'll manage without her for a few hours. As easy as that.

They choose a table in the beer garden and sit side by side, a polite distance apart. When the evening starts to cool, they ignore it, both of them needing the jackets neither has brought. It is harder to talk than it had been at the front gate. Harder to be themselves, here in the real world. Hazel and Dawn drink their drinks and look at the view, the straw-lined stripes of strawberry plants in the field opposite, the young people stacking baskets, locking up the little hut where they weigh the fruit and take the money. The fruit pickers are all teenagers, or just over, with sunburned noses and tanned arms. It is like watching a play, the ease of them, closing the farm gate, crossing the road to the pub, ready to turn the day's wages into pints of cold lager. Some of them nod to Dawn or say hello to her as they pull picnic tables together on the far side of the garden. Their presence changes the evening into something else, something noisy and alive. Dawn wonders if they are wondering who she is with. Why she is here.

"Friends of yours?" Hazel asks.

"Some," Dawn says. "I worked there for a few summers."

"Is that right? So you're a farmer?"

"That might be stretching it. See that sign on the gate? I painted that, believe it or not."

"The PICK YOUR OWN sign?"

"No, the PLEASE PAY BEFORE YOU EAT one."

"Bit of a killjoy," Hazel says. "Isn't scoffing them as you go half the fun?"

"Not if you're the farmer."

Hazel laughs so much at this that Dawn worries she is making fun of her. But she isn't laughing at her, she is listening to her, looking at her.

"I've always thought the 'Pick Your Own Strawberries' signs sound a bit bossy," Hazel says. "Sort of, 'I'm not picking strawberries for the likes of you; pick your own strawberries if you want them so much.'"

Hazel warms to her theme now, puts on her best farmer voice, a deep frown and a wagging finger. "Pick your own strawberries and then get off my land."

"Nobody round here sounds like that," Dawn protests. "Do we?"

Hazel shrugs. "I couldn't possibly say. Right." She puts a hand on Dawn's arm and grins. "I'm going to try it at the bar. See if they do 'Pull Your Own Pints.' Another?"

A week later Dawn asks Hazel if she'd like to come to the new aerobics class that has started in the church hall. They manage three classes but agree, in the end, that they're burning more calories suppressing giggles than they are doing the grapevine. One Saturday, Hazel says she'll tag along on market day, walking beside Dawn as she heaves Maggie's brown corduroy pushchair up the steep hill into town. When the shopping is done, Hazel treats them to milky coffees in the Co-op café, and they are both too slow to stop Maggie swiping a sugar cube from the bowl on the table. There's always something, a reason to meet up or call. Dawn gives Hazel a hand putting a fresh coat of paint on the front door. Hazel stops by after work with a book Dawn might like. It was good, everyone said, to see Dawn out and about, to see her making friends.

People tell stories

Dawn was sure that she talked more that summer than she had in the rest of her life put together. Hazel was full of stories. She talked and talked about her college friends, their posh names and eccentric habits. About hitchhiking through Greece during the holidays, about the fences she had climbed, or cut, in the name of peace and a bit of adventure. Protests were like parties, she told Dawn. All the buildup. All the people. Except they made you feel like you mattered, like you were doing something real. Hazel's stories weren't showing off, they were about sharing something, like telling a friend every detail of what happened in last night's *EastEnders* when they had missed it. Hazel was just catching Dawn up, as if surprised to find that she hadn't been there all along. Dawn's stories felt too quiet in comparison, gray and underwhelming. She had never been anywhere on her own, never lived anywhere but here. If she had stories at all, they were really Maggie's. The feeling, on the day Maggie was born, that she mattered at last, that she was needed in the world. The amazement she felt watching each new version of her, walking, talking, Maggie becoming herself. When Dawn actually talked about herself, she noticed, for the first time, that there were no spaces in her life, no gaps between school and work, or home and marriage. There hadn't been time for her to live through anything that might become a story worth telling. It was in August that Dawn realized it wasn't Hazel's haircut, or the things she talked about, that she liked. It was the way she changed the air as she moved through it.

Dawn had been thinking about buying the new jeans for a long time, just the right blue, the cut across her hips as if made for her. In the privacy of the shop's fitting room, she had stood between the mirror and the curtain and known it was the perfect outfit. But now, at home, looking at herself in segments reflected in the tiny bathroom cabinet, it wasn't the same. A glimpse of waist, an ankle if she stands on the side of the bath. She's not sure why it's bothering her so much. It's only a film. Dawn does her makeup carefully, sharpening her eyeliner pencil to a fresh point. She blots her best lipstick on a folded tissue. She lets herself enjoy it, the getting ready, the looking forward.

Her husband agrees with her, it's not his kind of film. She should go to the pictures with her friends. She should take the car, save them all waiting for the bus home. "Thanks," Dawn says. "I won't be late back."

The thick carpets of the cinema give Dawn a wobbly feeling in her legs, and she tries not to let it show. Hazel says they should go all out and buys a box of Maltesers to share. The cinema seems quiet for a Saturday night, their theater almost empty. "Maybe we've made an odd choice," Hazel says. "We should have gone for the boxing one after all." They sit in the middle of the middle, the place where friends sit, and watch the lion roaring, the theme music starting up over a movie-set Paris, the fakest of fake snow falling on the old-fashioned cars and streets.

Hazel cannot be the one to do it. She looks straight ahead, eyes fixed on the film, her right hand on her right thigh, an invitation. Dawn has lost track of this crazy film entirely now; she's not sure who is hiding in the wardrobe, who is under the bed. She can't keep up with which bits of the story are farce and which are sad. It would be easy, in the soft dark of the cinema, for Dawn to rest her hand on Hazel's, easy to sit, palm to palm, as if it were nothing.

It is a shock when it all stops, the lights suddenly bright as the credits roll, waking the audience up from strange dreams. On the walk back to the car, Dawn and Hazel talk about the film without pausing, how good it was, how the star's haircut was lovely, the music, the costumes, just right. The long summer day is over at last, darkening into night, and they are glad of the car, the radio playing, the warm air coming through the half-open windows. When Dawn turns off the engine, Hazel says, "Thanks for the lift; I really enjoyed the film," but she does not move to go. Dawn looks across at her and sees that her life, if she's not careful, will be made up of moments like this. All her chances to be alive slipping past. Because it seems an impossible gap to bridge, the final few inches between mouth and mouth, that it would take to kiss her. If she is wrong, if she has misread it, Dawn is sure she will lose it all. And if she is right? There will be an earthquake either way.

//////////

The sound of the car door closing leaves a silence behind it. Hazel's footsteps on the path, quiet, then quieter, then gone. Dawn, alone in the dark car, looks down at her shaking hands; shock, she supposes. She knew it was wrong, impolite at least, to make the comparison, his kiss, hers. The one, safe and familiar. And this, the rush and pulse of it, which must be visible on her face. Dawn looks at herself in the rearview mirror; she checks for signs of change.

SEPTEMBER 2022

Routine

Maggie sleeps with her arms thrown above her head like the laziest of ballerinas. She knows this because she wakes in this pose most mornings, with pins and needles in her hands and a pain between her shoulders. She knows it because Conor frequently complains about being hit in the face by a flailing arm in the middle of the night. When the alarm on her phone goes off, she reaches a hand down from the top of the pillow and taps snooze on the screen. When the alarm sounds again, she does the same. And once more. And one more time. When the alarm goes off a fifth time, she thinks of a parallel life where she might be heading into a morning yoga practice, instead of defrosting stiff muscles under a hot shower. She knows that if she is late, they are all late. Maggie gets up, she has children to cajole out of the house, she has herself.

Now she rushes. She thinks ahead. She sets the breakfast things on the kitchen table—cereal boxes, spoons—then hides herself in the bathroom with a satisfying click of the lock. She puts on her mascara as she pees. She will have to do. The mornings are ridiculous and they are ordinary. This is the life of a normal family, she tells herself. All of this is normal. As she puts on her coat, she hears it starting, some little war in the kitchen over which radio station should be playing. She does a quick mental calculation, how many years until the children might grow out of it, as she tries to ignore the rising voices. Conor is there, he can do the shouting, or appeasing, or whatever is needed this morning. There is nothing at all to stop her from walking through the door and making the earlier train. Except she cannot keep out of it. Some mixture of maternal guilt and superstition. Her fear of any of them leaving the house under a cloud, as if it will somehow invite tragedy, tempt fate.

Of course she goes back. She talks them down. She softens their full-voiced shouting to frown-faced sulking. Her son. Her daughter. Both quiet now and spooning cornflakes into their mouths in a begrudging truce. Then, Maggie checks she has her phone, her keys, she kisses all their heads goodbye. When she pulls the front door closed behind her, she sees the food waste bin, knocked over by foxes, its contents spread across the driveway. The eggshells and coffee grinds. The outer skin of a fennel bulb, which surely marks her out as a snob. There is no time to deal with it now, so she nudges the mess with the outside of her shoe into a pile by the hedge. Something else to come back to.

They called it, idiotically, the "summit meeting," and missing it was considered quite the office faux pas. Maggie checks the time in the corner of her laptop screen; she will still make the start of the meeting, just. But first she will have thirty-one minutes on the train, all to herself. This is Maggie's secret. The thing she does not tell any of them. The thing they would not understand if she did. When she takes the train into work, Maggie watches herself like a character in a film. She looks at her reflection in the train window and she dreams. She likes the commute, and she hates it, the glamour and the boredom of it. Sometimes she plays music through her wireless headphones and imagines people are looking at her, wondering who she is. She knows they are not. Maggie knows these journeys are essential in a way she could never fully explain. Each journey out a little leaving, each one home a safe return.

In the meeting, she listens to her colleagues speaking, she smiles and she nods. It'll be her turn next. Maggie sips her water, pinches the tendon, or whatever it is, between thumb and forefinger to wake herself up, to focus, then she moves to the front of the boardroom and clicks the mouse. She sets out her objectives for this quarter and people nod their heads, complicit in the idea that this is a legitimate way for grown adults to spend their time. It's all a great success. Maggie sits down and notes all the work she has agreed to do on her iPad, then she starts to delegate that work to other people. Her emails and messages reach out and touch base, they check in. The summit meeting ends, eventually, and there is lunch, then more emails, and several more conversations of varying degrees of pointlessness as the hours of the working day tick past her.

Maggie is on the concourse of Charing Cross Station when the thought hits her like jet lag. It is date night. Not a real date night with going out and new underwear, but the kind of date night people who have been married for almost twenty years might have, in their own house, while their children watch YouTube in an adjacent room. Conor is in charge of the food tonight, meaning, she's fairly sure, a hugely ambitious and impractical recipe. She knows there's no chance of dinner before nine, so she buys a KitKat to eat on the train. If he's cooking, she's responsible for entertainment. Maggie nibbles the chocolate from the edges of the wafer and scrolls through articles on her phone, looking for whatever the newest series is they were supposed to be watching. Best new shows streaming this month. What to watch if you loved this. She finds a true crime show she likes the sound of but worries it might be a bit gory. A third season of an American comedy they've watched before is a possibility. She reads reviews, weighing up the shortlist, she opens another link: The Top 100 New Shows You Can't Miss. It is exhausting. Maggie puts her phone in her bag, zipping it shut. They'll just have to have sex.

Date night is her own fault. She hadn't imagined that Conor would react as he did, that he would spring into action in defense of their marriage. She thought they had just been chatting, joking really, but Conor hadn't seen it that way, apparently. There were times when Maggie's straightforwardness was misunderstood as insensitivity. She took this, naturally, as a failure on the other person's part rather than as a hint to self-moderate. Maggie thought it was completely reasonable, healthy even, to tell her husband that she was bored of her life for nonspecific reasons.

"People don't stop wanting more, that's all I'm saying," she'd said as they were loading the dishwasher one evening.

But Conor had expected an explanation, or at least some specifics. Maggie had told him, clearly, she thought, that an affair was the last thing she'd want. She couldn't even imagine it, all the effort and energy it would take.

"I don't want to lose you, obviously," she'd explained. "It's just, a little flirtation. Everyone wants that." For the adrenaline of it, she meant, a moment of potential not acted upon. Opportunity but not action. When Conor looked at her, genuinely confused, she tried to retract it, brush the whole business off. But it was true, Maggie did want that again, just a moment with someone new, a tiny parcel wrapped in green leaves and tied with grass, fresh and perfect.

"Isn't that reasonable, normal even?"

"I don't know," Conor had said. "Is it?"

Maggie had tried again, to clarify.

"I don't want to sleep with anyone else, I just want to know that someone else might want to sleep with me."

It was the wrong thing to say, or at least she'd said it in the wrong way, and this meant she had date nights as well as summit meetings to deal with on the last Friday of the month.

The train tells Maggie exactly where she is. Coach five of a seven-coach train. Busy but on time. She sits next to the window and watches the trees and houses, the blur of city then suburbs wiping across her reflection. She watches the movie of herself returning home.

A beginner's guide to conversation

My door is always open," Heron likes to say, and so this afternoon Tom appears at the open back door half an hour after school finishes. Because tradition demands it, they eat tinned tomato soup and cheese on toast. Tom can't remember his grandfather cooking him anything else. It has become a running joke, a habit they are both too superstitious to deviate from.

They have a tin of soup between them, then another tin. Dipping and sipping at one end of the kitchen table. Heron washes up the soup bowls—he doesn't like to leave them—and says he'll go back into the garden, do the few bits that need doing. Tom says he'll help, or watch at least, from one of the plastic chairs just outside the back door. "You're never bored when you have a garden," Heron says, and Tom is sure that the exact opposite is true. He watches his grandfather, checking on the growing things he wants, pulling up the growing things he doesn't. He watches the way he appraises. The way he tucks away the spare loop of hose so that nobody trips. The way he sweeps the bit of patio beside the wheelie bin. As he works, Heron hums. A soundtrack to accompany the growing and rebelling of all the living things in the garden. Tom isn't doing any of that, although watching is a kind of doing too.

Heron makes tea in mugs with tractors on them. Tom knows that the tractors are Massey Fergusons because Heron has told him, probably hundreds of times. Tom doesn't like tea, but he drinks it, to be a man drinking tea with his grandfather. Heron hears his grandson take a breath, pause.

"Did you ever worry about the world?" Tom asks him. "When you were my age?"

The topic is somewhat more than Heron was expecting.

"The world?"

"You know," Tom tries again, "all of it. War. Politics. Climate change."

Heron thinks, swallows, and is forced to admit that, no, he didn't really. Not the climate change part anyway, which is exactly the point, he supposes.

"But I know what you mean. There's plenty to worry about, alright." Heron remembers his own grandfather, how he used to say, with irritating frequency, "If you have time to worry about other people's problems, you have few enough of your own." He had seemed to Heron a man of superhuman strength, hugely tall, mechanically operated somehow. He must have been born, when? 1904? 1905? The stuff of history books. Heron offers up his grandfather's words to Tom, passes them on for future use. They seem to please the boy, calm him even, and Heron feels he has done something useful with his day.

Before he leaves for home, Tom helps himself to another biscuit. They don't have a biscuit barrel at their house; his mum says they are old-fashioned and probably unhygienic. Old people's houses are always like this, Tom thinks, cozy, but too full. They don't know how to throw their stuff away. When Tom first started coming over after school, Heron would walk into the kitchen and simply ask him, "Have you ever used a hacksaw?" or, "Shall we change the fuse in this plug?" Had he any interest at all, Heron had asked him once, in climbing the stepladder to peep inside the birdhouse on the side of the garage? This is how they spent their hours together, fixing or making. Doing something with the stillness of a weekday afternoon.

Syntax errors

When Heron thinks about dying, he cannot get the grammar right. There is no tense in which to say I will miss being alive. Heron cannot find the words for thinking or the words for talking. He cannot tell his daughter or his grandchildren that he is ill, because he cannot work out how to say all the things he would have to say next. He cannot think of a way to explain that he has not finished with his life yet. He has not explained himself to them.

Mostly, Heron is fine because he is busy. He has the garden, and now the gym. When empty afternoons open up before him, he fills them with long-overdue jobs. He brings down boxes from the loft and sorts through old football programs, the negatives of photographs, kept for decades for who-knows-what reason. He thinks that the football programs might be worth something if he sold them online, relics of a different age. "Vintage," people called it. He spends a few hours on eBay, but can't decide, in the end, which would be worse: selling them or finding out nobody wanted to buy them.

It's the nights that are the problem. He cannot sleep. It's the medication, maybe, or all the thinking. On nights like tonight, when it is hopeless, Heron abandons his bed, slides his feet into neatly placed slippers, and walks himself to the kitchen. He takes the milk from the fridge and half fills his small Pyrex jug, a pleasing size for warming and pouring. It takes him three attempts to find the right button on the microwave. As the jug rotates, he chooses a mug, an impractical but cheering unicorn—his granddaughter's favorite.

Through the kitchen window, in the half-light of the not-yet-morning, Heron sees that his garden is more beautiful than he has ever known it. Full and green and heavy, ready for the change that is coming. He looks at the garden and makes a mental list of all the work waiting for his attention. The bay tree that needs reshaping. The ivy getting in around the garage door. All those leaves waiting to change and fall, the sweeping and composting that will keep him in a full-time job for weeks. Heron drinks his unicorn milk and finds that he is still surprised. That is the main feeling. A failing body was to be expected at some point. People get old, they get ill. Heron is nothing if not pragmatic. But he is surprised that it has changed him so quickly, made him into something fragile.

The sleepless nights might be bearable if he could just distract himself with a book, or one of those near-impossible jigsaw puzzles. But he is too tired for that, too unsettled. Trapped, between sleep and wakefulness with old conversations playing on repeat in his mind.

The doctor asking, "Are you sure you don't want someone here with you? Your wife?"

Heron, cornered into saying, "I'm divorced. Thirty, or is it forty, years."

That was a surprise, too, the imbalance he hasn't noticed building up. He has been divorced for so many more years than he'd been married. There should be a word for that. There probably was, in German, or Japanese. He will look it up.

"Your daughter, maybe?" the doctor had tried again.

"No. Really, I'm fine on my own. Please just—"

Until, in the end, Heron had asked the doctor, begged her, to just tell him the full version of the bad news. He had listened, making notes in his small spiky handwriting of all the words to look up later. The markers in his blood, the bone scans. A time span of not enough years. And then, he had driven to the supermarket and lost his mind for a few minutes in the frozen food aisle.

Heron thinks about what the doctor is doing now. He wonders how she manages it, carrying other people's bad news around with her all day. He hopes she had something lighter to deal with in her next appointment, a patient in remission, or something minor and easily fixed. He hopes that, after telling him he would die, she had a pleasant evening, one of those fancy ready-meals waiting for her at home. A family to eat it with.

He has not done enough, that is the trouble. He has not lived in all the ways available. He should have met more people. Tried things. He hasn't even traveled. He's been to France, obviously. Tenerife once or twice on a package deal when Maggie was at school. He won't now, he supposes, go to the places you see in movies. The Grand Canyon, Rome or wherever. If he told Maggie about the diagnosis, she would arrange it immediately, well-timed flights and well-priced hotels. Wherever he wanted to go. She would buy things and book things. She would take care of it all.

Sometimes he thinks about writing it down instead, handing her a Post-it Note that says: *I am ill.* Or composing a short series of text messages: *I am fine now but I will be ill, then iller. Two, maybe three years.* Things like that are easier said in writing. If he could just tell her she would know what to do, she would make it better. And then, she would make it worse, just by knowing. Heron feels sure that of all things, he cannot watch her watch him leave.

It will be morning soon; he may as well stay up. Make toast. Heron looks out the window at the garden he has made and thinks of all the days he has spent digging out paths and laying slabs. Stopping in the evenings to wash the first layer of dirt off at the garden tap. Carefully tidying the tools into their designated places in the shed, because a tidy workbench is a tidy mind. The insomnia is annoying; it is foolish. He knows something about himself that he has always known, just with a revised timescale, that is all. If he could sleep again, properly, it might all be different, clearer. Most nights he manages a few hours, sleeping deeply at first, his body shutting down, saving him. And then he wakes to a silent house, to his list of regrets in their various sizes. Nothing needs to change, the doctor had told him, not yet. But there was already so much work to it, the paperwork of appointment letters and referrals, the prescriptions and leaflets. All the administration of illness. The new fact of his dying, just another thing to do with his shopping every Thursday afternoon.

SEPTEMBER 1982

A wooden heart

They go to bed in the lunch hour, pulling blankets and pillows down onto the carpet to build a nest on the bedroom floor. They leave the curtains open so the neighbors won't have anything to notice. They slide the chain across the front door, and they shut out the whole world. Dawn is amazed by it still. The carpet against her shoulder blades. Her whole body given up to it. Or almost all. Dawn keeps one ear out of it. One ear, always listening. On guard.

The first time it happened, Hazel kissed Dawn's fingertips one by one and asked her why she didn't wear her wedding ring.

"It didn't fit me after I had the baby. They don't tell you about that. My feet have never been the same, either. A whole size bigger. I had to throw out my favorite boots."

Hazel had kissed her feet, too, toe by toe, and said, "Your feet are beautiful," and Dawn had laughed and squirmed her feet back under the covers.

"Give over, Hazel," she said. "Nobody's feet are beautiful."

Afterward, Hazel gets dressed, bra first, then knickers, which, Dawn says, is the wrong order. She watches as Hazel reassembles herself, solidifies. The way she brushes her hair, briskly, and without looking in the mirror. The way she picks up the gold can of hairspray from the dressing table and transforms. "Come on," Hazel says, "time to move," and she picks up Dawn's T-shirt from the floor, throws it into her lap. "Penny for them?"

And Dawn does want to tell Hazel her thoughts. She wants to tell her that she was just thinking how odd it is to be alive at last, at twenty-three. How funny it is. Or sad? But she can't say that. Instead, she smiles and says, "Nothing. No thoughts at all; you can save your money," as she turns her jeans from inside out to outside in.

Hazel leaves the flat first, the clicking of court shoes on paving slabs. The short walk back to her classroom, to the nine times tables and how the ancient Egyptians made papyrus. Dawn stays behind, pretending to do the cleaning. A bit of pin money, if anybody asks. Helping out.

Later, when she is doing something dull—ironing the sheets or standing in the queue at the butcher's—Dawn will play each note of this over again. The view of the top of Hazel's head as she kisses her way along the smile of scar beneath her belly button. Left to right. Hip to hip and back again. Before she leaves, she takes the furniture polish from under the sink and sprays huge swirls of Pledge into the air until the flat is filled with the scent of it. She pulls the front door closed behind her and slips the key under the mat, a perfume of fake pine forest left in her wake.

All the long hours, all the days

The post office queue is long that afternoon, and Dawn kicks herself for letting the day slip away from her again. When she finally makes it to the front, the woman behind the glass stamps the family allowance book and slides the notes and coins across the counter. She smiles at Dawn and says, as she does every week, "Into the purse, not the wallet, love," and Dawn smiles back as if these words are a necessary part of the exchange. As if the money is conjured up by the postmistress's magic spell, not the government. On the way to Maggie's playgroup, Dawn thinks about what she will spend it on this week, the bills Heron's wages don't quite stretch to, the bit she'll put aside for Maggie's winter coat. At the door, her little girl is waiting, all pink cheeks and overgrown fringe. She spots Dawn and unfolds her frown into a grin, holding both arms out from her sides, straight and stiff as justice. In her left hand, her empty lunchbox dangling from its plastic handle. In the right, something globular and hard to identify, made from modeling clay and sequins.

"A busy day!" Dawn says, and they walk, hand in hand, over the motorway bridge toward home. As they walk past the school they hear it, an opera of laughter and rhyming songs, skipping ropes slapping on tarmac. The sound of older children on the playground, washing over the wall and into the air around them. Dawn thinks of Hazel, leaning, whistle on a shoelace around her neck, scanning the yard for trouble like a sheriff.

There is teatime and bathtime and bedtime ahead of them. Through it all Maggie chatters, or she sings, or she asks Dawn why and what and how. There's a slight lull at teatime, her mouth briefly busy with baked beans and sausages cut into coins. In the bath, she starts again, and Dawn listens to three rounds of "The Farmer Wants a Wife." She inspects the tiny graze on Maggie's knee and agrees that the playgroup lady might have been a bit too liberal with the antiseptic, but it does look almost better already. When the work of the evening is done, they sit across from each other at the kitchen table, a mug of tea, a glass of milk, versions of the same person, available in different sizes. They arrange plastic farm animals on a tea tray. Sometimes Dawn lets Maggie break a shredded wheat into little bales of hay and they feed the plastic cows and the plastic horses. Dawn listens as Maggie updates her wish list for Father Christmas. It is, after all, the third week of September now. The little girl drops her hints heavily at her mother's feet, and Dawn picks them up, stores them away. She will order the doll that smells of strawberries, or cake, or whatever it is, before they sell out. Sometimes Heron is home before the child falls asleep. Not usually. He is a busy man.

None of it is easy for Dawn. The worrying is making her tired. Of course, the whole thing with Hazel is a secret; it has to be.

They have been so careful in their arrangements. Never waiting by the phone, always sticking to their stories, the evening classes, aerobics, the occasional shopping trip. Writing letters, Dawn had worried, was a step too far; it was too risky to put their feelings onto paper. But she needed the letters, the company they gave her when she was alone in the house. Dawn knows it is getting too big to keep from Heron. He's young, Hazel keeps reminding her, a modern man. They'll work it out like adults and make whatever arrangements need to be made. Life is chapters, Hazel says, or something like that. People start new ones. Turn pages.

Sometimes Dawn lets herself imagine that Hazel is right, that it will all be fine. He might understand, see it as a chance for him, too, to find something real, something more. Because Dawn does want to tell him; she wants to explain what this is and what it isn't. She married him because it was what they were supposed to do, that is all. People do that all the time; it wasn't wrong, she'll say, but it's hardly perfect, either. Both of them, she had always thought, felt gratitude more than anything else on their wedding day, a shared sense that their relationship was a shelter. Five years ago, the dress and the silk flowers had meant a license to blend in. A mortgage, a baby, all the things you needed to fill the days and years. But Dawn was a different person then, hardly a real person at all. Can she say that to her husband? In those words?

How would she begin to explain that this wasn't new at all but the opposite. Something she had always known, as deep and bright as bone.

Dawn takes down the child's shoebox she keeps in the far back corner of the linen closet. The lid held shut by a crisscross of rubber bands, the whole thing wrapped in a neatly folded pillowcase. She reads Hazel's letters over and over. The stories they write to each other, their modest fantasies. Dinner in a restaurant. Candlelight. Wine. Waking up together with an empty weekend ahead of them. A house by the sea with a scruffy dog they would walk together in the gloaming. None of it would happen, or could happen, unless, or until, she tells him. She will tell him tonight. Or she will carry on like this forever, a frayed little tightrope of a life. Dawn thinks. She worries. She stacks her Tupperware and bleaches her whites. She keeps the kitchen just so.

Dawn knows she will never make herself understood, not fully. People will only think of the sex. Skin and sweat. But the real cheating hasn't happened in bed; Dawn knows that. The worst of it has happened in the few moments of real life they have made together. Hazel, washing up their coffee cups as Dawn slid her hands into the back pockets of her jeans. Walking in the park, holding hands when they were sure nobody was looking, playing at a life they would never have. The way they listened to each other; the way they argued and made up.

Words are said

She has cooked him his favorite, chops and chips, and between mouthfuls he tells her about his day. The big order coming in. The new apprentice they've taken on in the warehouse who calls him Mr. Barnes, as if he is an old man.

"Twenty-five is an old man when you're sixteen, though, isn't it?"

And she almost loses her nerve then, because he is lovely, but not, she is quite sure, in love with her, any more than she is with him. After dinner he takes a screwdriver and tightens up the spice rack on the kitchen wall. Keeping on top of it all, pulling his weight. He washes his hands with Fairy Liquid at the kitchen sink. He checks the football pools. Dawn sees he has a hole in his right sock where his big toe is poking through. He is still like a boy sometimes, waiting for his mother to fix his problems for him. But he has a wife now, he has Dawn. The sock is her fault.

In the evenings, he likes to talk about what their life together will become. Grandchildren visiting, the allotment he will have. He thinks it is romantic, pinning down the future, his prophecy of contented old age. Dawn listens to his plans with the air squeezed out of her lungs. Not yet, not yet, she thinks. Let me be young first.

Once the dust has settled, Dawn will draw up a neat little timetable with straight lines, listing out the days their daughter will stay with her, the days she will stay with him. It's not unknown, it's normal even. That is what she will say.

She tidies away the last of the day and says to her husband, "Something has happened. Something is happening."

She tells him all of it, just as she has practiced. She explains, carefully, slowly, in the low voice she uses in the evening so she won't wake their daughter. But it is not as she planned. Heron's face, his voice when he eventually uses it, are not as Dawn has planned at all.

The nuclear family

He does not want her in their bed, which is fair. But the sofa is too small, and too far away from Maggie if she calls out in the night. So Dawn spreads blankets on the landing floor to make her bed. Each morning, she packs them away before her daughter wakes up.

Before she opens her eyes Dawn can hear him, the scrape, dip, water-shake of his shaving on the other side of the bathroom door. The humming, which she thinks at first is a hymn, then recognizes as the tune from a radio jingle advertising credit cards. She listens to his sounds bouncing off the bathroom tiles, the stubbly scum that will gather in a tidemark around the sink. Soon he will come out of the bathroom and she will go in. She will wipe the sink clean, soap her flannel, begin her day. Or she might just lay where she is, flat on the floor, a moth-eaten tiger skin rug with glass eyes and sharp teeth. She could stay here, still and silent, letting them all walk along the boneless skin of her back.

Dawn dresses her daughter for the weather. She pours milk on her Weetabix and wets the corner of a tea towel under the kitchen tap to rub a yogurt stain from the child's cardigan because there isn't a cleaner one left in the house. She makes sandwiches, ham, and for a treat, hides a Penguin bar underneath them. She thinks of the little girl, opening the clasp of her lunchbox in a few hours' time, the way she will find the chocolate, the way it will make her remember her mother.

Dawn calls up the stairs, "It's time to go. Let's get your shoes on."

But Maggie doesn't reply, or rather her silence does. That, and a little scuffle coming from Dawn and Heron's bedroom. She should be furious at all the mess. Her best lipstick slightly gnawed, the tip broken off and squished into the dressing table. Powder everywhere. But Maggie is so proud of herself, admiring her reflection in the mirror, wearing every necklace and bangle Dawn owns. Somehow Dawn manages to smile. She manages to say, "You look like a movie star, Mags. Let's see if we have any film in the camera. We can take a photo for Daddy."

When Maggie is at playgroup, the wrong kind of quiet fills the house. But they must send her, Heron is sure about this. To prepare her for school, to make sure she learns how to fit in, how to share. When Maggie is at playgroup, Dawn is meant to be busy. Instead, she mopes. Instead, she misses her. When she is gone, Dawn tries to picture Maggie in her mind's eye. To hold her there. Sitting in a circle on the cold hall floor, her fingers a spider climbing up a spout. Maggie, frowning in the way she does when lost in concentration, elbow-deep in sugar paper and dry macaroni. The women who run the playgroup say she likes the home corner best, playing Mummies and Daddies, tucking her plastic baby in for a well-earned nap. Wielding the little wooden iron. Maggie plays, and Dawn counts the hours left in the day.

Dawn sits on the edge of her daughter's bed and tries not to think about her. She tries not to think about Hazel, either. About ways to see her or phone her, to tell her that he knows. To ask her what on earth they are supposed to do now. Instead, she climbs under the covers and listens to the sounds of the empty house. The birds outside. The washing machine spinning. She turns to face the wall and sees the shape of Antarctica, scratched out of the wood chip wallpaper by Maggie's tiny fingernails. Then she falls asleep, surrounded by her daughter's claw scratchings, by the smell of her child's head left behind on the pink cotton pillowcase.

Later, Heron and Dawn will wait, until their neighbors have turned off their bedside lamps, checked the radio alarm clock is set, the back door locked, and the cat called in. Only then, when everything around them is quiet and still, will they let it begin again. This same fight, repeating. Accusations thrown in whispers so they won't wake Maggie, so they won't make a scene. He cares too much about what other people think, Dawn says. His mother. The blokes at work. This is about his pride. Heron uses the words Dawn has been expecting. Disgust. He says, "You disgust me."

Which is just a cliché, she thinks. It is simply the obvious thing to say to her now.

He asks her the same questions he asked the night before and the night before that, stuttering, still surprised. Why and how she could have done it. "Don't you love me?" he asks, over and over. "I thought we loved each other."

She tries to hunt down a way to explain.

"This is different. It's not the same."

He asks about the sex, that is expected.

"It's not the same," she says.

There is something new about the arguing tonight, something else is fueling him. Some new clarity that he has been betrayed. Heron is so angry that Dawn thinks she might laugh, not at him exactly, but at the intensity of his rage, how cartoonish it is. She does not recognize this version of him, these new poses, fists clenched, head in his hands.

"I just can't believe I married a—"

They cannot keep going like this. The same fight, the same insults. Tonight, Dawn thinks she can feel it changing, tipping over into a conclusion they can't come back from. Maggie is asleep. She is safe. Heron wouldn't hurt her, Dawn is sure of that. But she's not nearly so sure about herself. Not tonight. Everyone has their limit, she thinks, even Heron. A breaking point when they do things they never thought possible. "We need a breather," Dawn says, "a night off before things go too far." He nods, he deflates, just a little, because even like this he can see she is right. "You stay," Dawn says, and she takes the car keys from the hook, her coat from the banister, and is gone.

There is nowhere to go at this time, in this place, so she drives to the little car park opposite Maggie's playgroup and tells herself she will be safe there, even in the dark. She cranks the driver's seat back to a slope and presses down the door lock

button, her coat making do as a blanket. The weather is turning, shifting to autumn, but the car is no worse a bed than the
landing carpet. Heron will assume she has gone to Hazel's,
but she can't show up there without warning, not at this time
of night. Turning up on the doorstep with only her handbag,
the keys to a car that isn't strictly hers. It would only take one
old dear looking out the front window to send gossip flying
around the village, or worse, the school gates. Perhaps he will
hope she has driven to the ends of the earth and disappeared.
He probably wouldn't mind which it is as long as she's gone.
But Dawn can't go to any of those places. She can't go anywhere without Maggie.

She wakes just before six, the light of the day flooding the
car. She does what she can to look presentable, fingers comb-
ing out curls, wiping mascara smudges from under her eyes
with a swipe of each thumb. She will drive the few minutes
home before anyone sees her, slip the car onto the drive and
herself into the house. She will be there when Maggie wakes
up, standing at the kitchen counter, cutting the crusts from her
daughter's toast as if nothing has happened. It will be a bright
day, one of the last before the season changes properly. There
is hope on a morning like this. Heron has said his piece, and
she has suffered a night out in the cold. Surely, that is enough.

Dawn turns the car onto their road and passes the milk-
man coming in the opposite direction, the battery buzz and
glass clinks of his float. He sees plenty, she thinks. Tries not
to. Dawn closes the car door softly, the day already starting to
warm, and steps on the mess the locksmith has left behind, a
dusting of wooden sand on the front doorstep.

OCTOBER 2022

Pay to exit

There are appointments, lots of them, and Heron worries a great deal about the hospital parking arrangements. The instructions on hospital parking machines, he has observed, are always inexplicably complex. Insert ticket this way up. Scan this, tap here, proceed to car. He does not enjoy the feeling of a queue building up behind him. Impatient patients and their visitors stacking up as he fumbles with his contactless card. Not to mention the quiet insult of having to pay to leave your car while they check your bones for cancer.

The doctor explains it to him again. They already know what it is and where it is. They even know what to do about it. But they need to watch it, stalk it to see if it plans to spread to some other hidden part of his body. Heron sits in a plastic chair and a nurse fits the cannula into the back of his hand. Her touch is too gentle, light fingertips against the skin of his wrist and inner elbow and he flinches, not from pain, but from tickles. There is a polite formality to the whole procedure, a kindness which he worries might make him tearful. Strange, how sympathy is so hard to bear. Only the radiologist uses the actual word, everyone else seems to avoid it, like superstitious actors. It is for his benefit, Heron thinks, to protect his feelings, or maybe just to keep him calm before the scan. He wonders if he ought to give his permission, tell them it's okay to say it as they see it. But it seems to be a rule among them, and he doesn't like to interfere.

The doctor has told Heron not to look up his symptoms online, not to let his imagination run away with him. He knows, or has heard at least, how easy it is to get the wrong end of the stick.

"Does it hurt? The scan," he asks the nurse, and they are both a little surprised to hear him speak.

"Not at all," she reassures him. "Some people don't like the feeling of being in there; it's a bit of a tight squeeze. Just listen to the music, Henry, and it'll all be over before you know it."

"Everyone calls me Heron," he tells the nurse. Henry sounds strange, not his anymore.

"As in the bird?" the nurse asks. Heron has been Heron for as long as he can remember. Renamed by his baby brother who couldn't quite manage Henry. The name had stuck to him then, as names do.

The nurse looks her patient up and down, this beaky man, gray hair swept back from his forehead. His legs long and thin, with the top half starting to unbalance him, his abdomen puffing out with a steroid plumpness.

"It suits you."

They inject a dye into his veins to help them see whatever it is they will see. He must, the nurse insists, wear earplugs or headphones.

"It's loud in there," she says. "Very."

"We can play whatever you like, patient's choice," the radiographer chirps through the intercom. Every other person in this room, Heron thinks, is thirty years too young to have heard of Hall and Oates.

"Whatever you like, I'm not fussy, really," he says. "Nothing classical."

They fix him into place with foam shapes, a wedge under his head, a large sausage of a cushion under his knees. Stay as still as you can, they tell him.

"Try," they say, "to relax."

Heron is glad he didn't choose any music; the music they play for him is just right. Somebody's machine, or something. He closes his eyes and listens to the singer's voice, soft but serious. He tries to catch the lyrics. Killer whales. Rabbit hearts. The music is good, he thinks, it is the kind of music that might take your mind elsewhere, to another time and place altogether, if you were willing to go.

Reliable sources

Maggie had read it in a magazine, years ago, the theory that the car was the place to talk to your teenage children. Something to do with the forced intimacy of it, the impossibility of escape. She switches on the engine and her son reaches out a hand to adjust the volume on the radio. In reply, she sets the windscreen wipers waving. Water and rubber squeaking across the glass, although the window is clean enough. He moves his seat back an inch. She adjusts the heat, just slightly. They are the same. The siren call of buttons and dials. The need to control.

They drive past the petrol station on the ring road, the council swimming pool, its blue and white water slides overhanging the car park. Maggie notices the dry cleaners on the corner has closed down and opens her mouth to tell Tom, then shuts it again. Because he will find the observation pointless, sigh in that way he does as if insulted to have something so banal brought to his attention. Or worse, as she's noticed lately, he might humor her with some polite acknowledging sound. Smirking at the insignificant details she notices. The things that matter only to her.

Instead she says, "Do you know what you're going to ask him?"

"Questions. The teacher's given us a list."

"What sort of questions?" Maggie keeps trying. She keeps talking.

"Questions, Mum. Just normal questions."

"It's for school. History," Tom had explained to his grandad over the phone, and Heron had thought, there's a milestone; one minute it's a bus pass, the next you're the subject of a history project.

"I'm not sure I've got much to tell you, but we can give it a go. Saturday morning?" He is pleased, in truth, to have something different to do. Lately, Heron has started to feel he is wasting days. He suspects he should be finding meaningful things to do, painting with watercolors, or looking at the sea, not just keeping his patio clear with the new leaf blower.

By the time Maggie and Tom pull up at the house, Heron has everything set out and ready—a plate of sandwiches, the two big photo albums down from the shelf. It is strange, Heron thinks, how your own life never feels like history. It doesn't take long, though, your children, your children's children, looking at the clothes you wore, the thoughts you thought, as if they are relics in a glass case.

Tom throws his coat over the banister and realizes, far too late, that he could have just kept quiet about the homework and made up all the answers. Interviewing old people was the kind of thing his history teacher really went in for. "History is happening now," Mr. McAlpine was always saying, which confused Tom. History has already happened, he thought, wasn't that the whole bloody point?

"You'll be amazed," his teacher had said, "how much there is to learn from the people in your own family." Although it was, he had to admit, much easier back when grandparents had a war to talk about.

"Ask them if they remember the three-day week," Mr. McAlpine had said, and Tom was sure he was joking, making it up to test them, like a left-handed hammer or tartan paint, until he googled it in the car on the way over.

"I'm about your age there," Heron says, handing Tom a photograph, "a bit older, maybe."

On the back someone had written *Old Kent Road, 1974*, in blue Biro, pressing down with the pen a bit too hard, so the bumps of the words had raised up on the image like braille.

Tom holds the picture by its rounded corners, all the colors brownish as if soaked in tea. It is a photo of a smiling boy, dark hair down to his collar. Tom has never imagined Heron without white hair. He opens his lever arch file and sets his phone to record, just as the teacher has told him to. The questions are just questions, about what school was like in the olden days. Questions about how much and if Heron remembers the events the history textbook thinks he ought to know. Strikes. Prime ministers. Things like that. Heron tells Tom that, when he was in school, teachers would hit the small children with a slipper, bigger ones with a stick, and again Tom isn't sure if he's joking. Heron tries to describe a slide rule, sort of like a calculator, but not quite. He explains that there was TV, but not nearly as much. Records and then tapes and then CDs. He tells him about buying his first car, about how many people you could get into it, before there were seat belts. No mobile phones. People wrote letters, or, he realizes it's hard to believe, they actually talked to each other, face-to-face.

"And"—Tom is squirming a bit now; he's not sure if he should skip over this part—"it's about getting married and stuff," he says.

"It's fine. I was married once, you know that of course. You can ask."

"Okay." Tom looks down at the photocopied worksheet. "How did you meet?"

"A dating app," Heron says.

Tom rolls his eyes; it's not funny, or he won't admit that it might be.

"We just met, I suppose. We'd both only just left school. I was an apprentice and I cut my hand mucking about with something or other. She was behind the counter at the chemists when I went in for some plasters. How's that for romantic?"

Tom tries to smile; he knows he should. Then he ticks the marriage question off the list and moves quickly on to the next one.

Maggie, in the kitchen, puts down the plate she is drying and stops, caught in the beam of this story she hasn't heard before. She listens to her son asking the questions she has never been able to ask and reminds herself to breathe.

Tom thinks he is finished, or wants to be, but his grandad keeps talking and he's not sure how to stop him. Heron is in full flow now, memories he hasn't called up for decades, remembering a person he hasn't been for years. A man-boy who cared about how his hair looked, who bothered to shrink his Levi's in the bath to the perfect fit. It seems impossible to think of himself as a person whose only real problem was worrying if the girl he liked knew he was alive. "I took her to pubs," he tells Tom. "The kind you could take a girl to, you know. We liked each other. We were both quiet and we could be quiet people together." Tom listens, what choice is there? He nods.

"I asked a bloke I worked with to be best man, because I couldn't choose between my two brothers. It was all, just normal. Just as I'd hoped or expected it would be. Then we had your mum and all that began, the nappies and the bottles. You'll be in college probably at that age, not bathing a baby in the kitchen sink. Or you'd better be."

Tom blushes at this, embarrassed at the idea of himself as a father, as a grown person.

And what next, Maggie wills them both from the next room. What next?

Her son. Her father. Talking as if she isn't there, as if she isn't the punch line to the story they are telling. Maggie listens and she cannot seem to move. One foot twitching, ready to rush in, to be part of it. The other, glued to the floor, keeping her in place, trying not to break the spell.

There are topics not talked about for so long they become impossible to say out loud. Maggie thinks of her parents' marriage in a lost language, in words she has not heard or used for years. She doesn't have the vocabulary now to ask her father these questions, how they met, how they split up. She only has a tourist's grasp of the language when she needs to be a poet. Maybe Tom is just the right person to do it for her, the buffer of a generation allowing him all of the curiosity but none of the pain. Maybe he can ask Heron the practical things, the when and how and why questions about her mother that she has never been able to.

Maggie stays in the kitchen. She listens and she waits. She finishes the drying up and hears her son say, "There's a last question. It's, 'Do you have any advice for me?'"

Tom could write the answer to this without asking. Always hold the door open. If in doubt, wear a tie. Old-fashioned nonsense like that that his grandfather is always coming out with. Heron looks across at the boy in the chair opposite, his hair flopped across one eye. This boy who hasn't begun yet. He wants to say, you will be so many people in your lifetime that you'll look back one day and not even recognize some of the people you have been. Heron looks at his grandson, his pen poised over his homework.

"Just do what you think is best, Tom. That's all you can ever do."

This is a lullaby

That night, Tom hears his mother on the landing, the creak of old floorboards under new carpet. He listens as the footsteps stop at his sister's bedroom door, the sound of the handle turning, the pause as she looks in to check on Olivia. The footsteps starting up again, for him.

Maggie always knocks these days, because Tom insists upon it, growls really, at anyone who crosses the threshold without his permission. She moves in a sweep around the room, gathering and tidying. She throws an armful of discarded T-shirts into the laundry basket, straightens some textbooks into a neat rectangular pile on the desk. Some order put to the room, Maggie walks over to the bed, reaches out a hand to smooth her son's hair, then plumps his pillows. Tom likes it. He pretends not to, leaning away from her touch. He unsettles his hair again with a shake of his head, erasing the marks of her care.

And normally she would leave it, let it all be just as he wants. But tonight she says, "Go on. Let me look after you. For a treat."

Because she likes it too, this chance to fuss over him, just for a moment. To let it all back in. "Anyway," his mother says, "you'll be looking after me soon enough. It's why I'm always nagging you to do your homework. I need you to earn the big bucks so you can afford the fancy old-people's home for me and Dad."

Tom smiles now, in spite of himself, and shakes his head.

"Second-best old-people's home maybe. One where they have a real piano for you to sit around singing songs from the war."

"Charming. I think I'd better call the school, see if they'll send over some extra history homework. And maths."

This is how it can be.

A truce between mother and son, a peace settling between them that will last the night.

OCTOBER 1982

Soft-boiled

Maggie sits patiently in her Care Bear pajamas and waits for her father to know what to do.

Heron has exhausted all his options. The usual babysitter is laid low with glandular fever, her O-Levels hanging in the balance. Even Linda next door, usually so reliable, can't help him today. She has her hands full with her own, the house awash with children for half term. Heron will have to manage, find a way.

"An egg? I can boil you an egg?"

She shakes her head.

"Cornflakes?"

Maggie shakes her head again and crosses her arms. She looks as if she might cry, or tip the table over and start a bar brawl. It is unbelievable that such a small girl can be so strong-willed. So unbending. Heron has changed his mind. He thinks he has. Now he has thought about it, he wonders if he has gone about this all wrong. Nobody needs to know. It can all be put behind them. Forgotten. He can forgive Dawn. It's not as if she had a real affair. She is just lonely, he thinks, in the way wives can be. She needs something for herself, a part-time job. Another baby.

Heron calls the office and says he has a stomach bug, maybe an ulcer, sowing the seed of something time-consuming in case he needs it later. Then he makes his daughter toast. When she cries at the squares, he makes the toast again, but in triangles. He is doing his best, better than many men would do in his place. He has not thrown his wife out onto the street, exactly. He has not cracked her ribs or pinned her to their bed. He is not that kind of husband. He will forgive her, and their lives will go back to normal. He has decided.

"Let's get dressed. It's getting late."

Heron knows Maggie does things in the day, he just isn't sure what or when. It might be a playgroup day, or the day Dawn takes her to the coffee morning at the library. It doesn't matter.

"Here, Maggie, let's put this on."

He tries to peel up Maggie's pajama top, but she clamps her arms to her sides.

"You don't like this dress?"

"No." Her little face, thunder. Fury.

"This one?"

"No."

He empties Maggie's drawers onto the bedroom carpet. Tartan dresses and soft dungarees. Her favorite Rupert the Bear jacket. The lot. With each rejected T-shirt, Heron feels his patience draining out of him. He will snap, he can feel it coming. Any minute now he will pick up this tiny person and dress her in something, anything. He whispers it to himself, the reminder that she is only three. She is only three.

"What is it that you want, Maggie? We've been through nearly all your clothes."

"I want Mummy."

Heron is surprised he has remembered her surname, this woman who was barely in his peripheral vision a few months ago. He leaves Maggie eating her toast and flips the telephone directory open, sliding his finger from top to bottom, tiny black letters, bible-thin pages. Walker, Weekes, Wright. Wright, H. It is Dawn who picks up the phone, a relief of sorts, and she agrees, it can't go on like this. Yes, they must talk; yes, she will meet them at the park. Half an hour. Now. As soon as possible.

They take turns pushing their daughter on the swing. Forward and back. Forward and back.

"When I'm growed up," Maggie says, "Mummy will be a little girl."

And Dawn pushes and waits, pushes and waits, and says, "No, not quite like that, love. You only grow up, not down."

They push the swing together, Heron at her back, Dawn at the front, pretending to snatch her welly boots from her feet each time she rises up toward her. When Maggie has had enough, the three of them sit on the bench together and share the thermos of hot chocolate Dawn has brought, the little Tupperware box of cream crackers, as if nothing at all has happened to them.

"Cheers," Dawn says, raising the lid of the flask to him.

"Cheers," he says in reply. Tapping the corner of his cracker to the edge of her cup.

Maggie nibbles on her snack, and Heron and Dawn talk in the way parents do in front of a small child. Editing vocabulary that might be repeated, treading in delicate footsteps through their conversation.

"She needs me," Dawn says. "We need each other." She is quiet. Fierce.

"I know. I do know." Heron pauses now, tries to think. "Actually, can you take her now? I need to go to work."

"If you give me a key."

So he does.

It is like signing a treaty, although nobody is quite sure of the terms. Dawn will take Maggie back to the house, she will need her lunch soon, her afternoon nap. Heron will make a miraculous recovery and go back to work. The last thing any of them need is for him to lose his job. They don't talk about where Dawn will sleep that night or who will take Maggie to playgroup in the morning. It is progress all the same, a step forward. Heron checks his watch, says he'll make it to the office by half past if he hurries. He'll say there was traffic.

"In a while, Crocodile," he says to Maggie, tapping a finger to the tip of her nose.

"Bye-bye, Alligator!" she shouts, standing on the bench, waving and jumping until he is out of sight.

Hard

The solicitor's office is above a dry cleaner's, at the cheap end of the high street. Heron presses the buzzer beside the door and a woman's voice tells him to come up the stairs, two flights. He has been here before, although not for years, to sign paperwork for the house. Conveyancing, through the door on the left. Today, he's here for the door on the right, family. Heron waits for his appointment and the secretary makes him a coffee, scraping the last granules from the bottom of the Nescafé jar. When she asks, he says, "White please, no sugar," which he regrets when he sees her splash UHT milk into the mug. The coffee tastes of plastic; it tastes of camping. He keeps making mistakes like this, small errors of judgment that spoil things. He drinks the coffee and tries to put it behind him. He'll know for next time.

He'd booked the appointment a week ago. There was no harm, surely, in finding out what a solicitor has to say about it all. Heron wants information, that's all; he wants to know what he is supposed to do now. What the rules are. The office is full of filing cabinets, certificates on the wall. It is the kind of office that changes Heron's voice, just slightly. When the solicitor asks him questions, Heron takes the edge off his accent. He takes care to describe Maggie as "three," not "free."

It is warm in the office, and the solicitor has draped his suit jacket over the back of his chair. His shirtsleeves puff out at the elbow above springy gold sleeve garters, and Heron wonders about them, what purpose they serve. If they are uncomfortable to wear. When the solicitor speaks again, Heron jumps slightly at the intrusion on his thoughts.

"Don't worry. In cases like this," the solicitor says, "the court almost always awards custody to the father."

The solicitor talks, and Heron finds it is reassuring to sit in front of this man in his striped tie, his name in brass on the door. A man who knows exactly what he should do. His mother was right, they needed a professional. It was all too much, she had said, for Heron to manage on his own. Too complicated. This isn't his first case of this sort, the solicitor explains. Although, as he said on the phone, "You normally only see this sort of thing in London. Anyway, the case for an unfit mother writes itself."

"Unfit?" Heron repeats it.

"Judges are pretty clear." The solicitor lists the reasons on thick fingers. "Risk to the child, psychological harm, influence of, well"—a clearing of the throat as he rearranges his mouth to say—"perversion."

It's a good case. Plenty of work, the divorce, the custody claim, probably an appeal. But he's just not convinced this young man has the stomach for it. The solicitor recalibrates, offers the alternative, although it is like watching money walk out the door.

"You can always try going off the books, if that would suit you better. When there's a, what shall we call it, a bit of scandal? The other party can often be persuaded to pull a disappearing act before there's a fuss. Avoid it ending up in the papers."

Heron speaks now, checks he understands what this man is telling him.

"You think I should blackmail my own wife?"

The solicitor doesn't sigh, but he wants to. It is almost lunchtime, and he has a list as long as his arm to get through. Why, he wonders for the third time that day, do people come in here asking for advice they don't want to take? He is not unsympathetic, of course he's not. This man has been through a terrible shock; you can see that just by looking at him. Still. He leans forward on his desk and asks the questions Heron is too afraid to ask himself.

"Does she even want the child now? This"—the solicitor pauses in search of the word, swallows back "affair" and finds "situation"—"has clearly been going on for months. It's my guess your wife is far from interested in family life anymore." Then a pause, to make the point. "If you don't sue for full custody of your daughter, social services will take care of the decision for you."

Before he leaves, Heron writes a check, enough to cover the first meeting and to pay for whatever needs doing next. He tells the solicitor everything he knows: that Dawn is living there now, with that woman; that she admitted it all, told him to his face, at his own kitchen table. He tells the secretary, too, who has listened to every word, eyes averted, taking her notes in the dash-dot code of shorthand. Something has started now, he knows that. All the processes and people who will turn his private problems into something official. The new threat hanging over him, that they would take Maggie away if he didn't do as he was told. Heron is not unburdened by this meeting, these people have taken something else from him besides their fee. They have made it true.

NOVEMBER 2022

It's the paperwork that does it in the end

Heron needs to arrange power of attorney, not immediately, the doctor says, but at some stage. When he feels ready. Soon. He will have to tell her.

They are normally on let-yourself-in terms, dropping in unannounced with a bit of news, the exchange of small objects from him to her and her to him. Seedlings from his greenhouse, some little freebie from work she thinks he'll make use of. Maggie walks in and out of Heron's house as if she never quite left it, visiting but never a guest. Today, he had actually called to invite her, asked if she'd come without the children, which means, she imagines, something.

Heron and Maggie sit on opposite sides of his kitchen table, warming palms against mugs. They chat about the reliability of the BBC Weather app, whether those boiling water taps are really worth the outlay when kettles seem perfectly capable. It is exactly how other people think of them. At ease in each other's company. Content. And it is true, the easiness of it all is beautiful. It's the pointing it out that spoils things. It has always annoyed Maggie, people telling her how lucky she is to have this, their way of being together. You're so lucky, they say, to be so close to your father.

"Lucky," people said, when they really meant "strange." As if being raised by just your dad is the next rung up from being raised by wolves. As if a father and daughter living alone was so unusual it had to be mentioned, a rare little alpine plant among the common or garden-variety families. Maggie wasn't even sure it was true, not strictly. There were always other people around, helping out. The real aloneness, she thinks, didn't start until her grandmother died, when Maggie was twelve. Then it really was just the two of them. Just Heron and Maggie, their strange, unbreakable little family.

Maggie says she has two hours, then Olivia needs to be collected from her football match and redelivered to an under-the-sea-themed birthday party. Until then, she can sit in the worn-in comfort of Heron's small talk, waiting for him to explain the cardboard box of papers on the kitchen table.

She thought it would be something like this: one of his little projects, which, as usual, looks like it has already started to get out of hand. Heron is never happier than when he has a project on the go and Maggie is well-used to being dragged in for administrative support. He'll want help with a website, probably, some form that needs filling in. It reminds her of his competitions phase, when he won a year's supply of fabric softener or whatever it was. Or the time he got so worked up about the state of grass verges, she'd had to tell him to rein it in before the local MP put him on some kind of cranks watch list.

"Alright then. What have you got for me?" she asks, peering into the box. "A petition against petitions?"

"I'm having a sort-out," Heron tells her. "Can you take anything you want? I'll get rid of the rest."

Maggie flicks through all the paper nonsense she should have cleared out years ago—gymnastics certificates and school reports. French exercise books that betray an ongoing struggle with the past participle. She works through her pile, and he works through his. Keep. Recycle. Recycle. Keep.

They are both the kind of people who would scoff at the very idea of meditation. In fact, Maggie is known to have gone on fairly long rants about what she considers the pernicious cult of mindfulness. But here they are, together, deep in the peaceful satisfaction of working on a long-overdue task.

"It's amazing, isn't it?" Maggie says. "Unbelievable. How much you accumulate."

"It is," Heron agrees, "unbelievable," as he feeds ten-year-old bank statements into the shredder. This, in fact, is the luck other people see in them. The luck of having someone who will listen to you saying all the dull things, obvious and true, which nonetheless seem important enough to say out loud. How much paperwork there is in living a life. How amazing it is to see it, to hold it in your hands.

They laugh at the pile of *Which?* magazines, at the instruction manual for a toaster that was three toasters ago. Expired checkbooks from accounts that don't exist anymore. From banks that don't exist anymore.

"Hoarding," Maggie says. "You know this is hoarding."

But Heron doesn't want to hold on to any of these things. He wants the space their absence will create, in his house and in his mind. Later, when Maggie is gone, he'll finish the job. Shred the folder he stuffed behind the microwave when she arrived, recycle the archive box in the loft. It wouldn't be fair, he thinks, to leave that job behind him.

"Is that it, then?" Maggie asks when they have finished. "No hidden premium bonds or treasure maps lurking any- where?"

Heron walks the few steps across the kitchen to the small corkboard beside the back door. He lifts up a menu for a Chi- nese takeaway, and from behind it, unpins a letter on hospital- headed paper. Maggie reads it, once, twice. *Dear Mr. Barnes . . . Next appointment . . . Oncology.* Maggie reads the letter and understands that her father will die. This is it then; this is the next thing. Not a shock exactly, but a confirmation. She feels her understanding float up to the surface. A piece of deeply held knowledge she has been storing without meaning to. U2 song lyrics, the date of the Battle of Hastings, her father's mortality. All of it information held by her body, whether her brain wants to keep it or not. Maggie hands back the letter and watches Heron pin it on the board.

"I see," she says, because she does.

Afterward, they sit down again. The same people they have always been. Sitting at the same table. New information leav- ing a vapor trail across their conversation. Maggie doesn't ask questions about second opinions or timelines. Heron offers nothing more in the way of detail. They do not joke or cry or do any of the things it is usual or useful to do at a time like this.

Instead, Heron makes more tea and Maggie slips old photos into new albums. A version of herself, about two years old, ice cream dripping down her chin. At three-ish, red lipstick smeared across her cheeks, strings of beads around her neck. All the usual photographs of a life. Her first day of school. Brownie camp.

Maggie had planned to talk to Heron today about Olivia's bedroom door, its stiff handle. See if he'd pop over to take a look. Normally, her dad would arrive to Sunday lunch with his toolbox, knowing some small job would be waiting for him. She had caught him before, scouring the house, looking for loose hinges or dead light bulbs, unable to resist his compulsion to be useful. You couldn't ask a man with cancer to fix a door handle for you.

There were things she should say, Maggie knew that, to ease them both through this moment, to move them back into the mundane but necessary place of a Saturday afternoon in November. The trouble was, words were never really the way to get through to Heron. The things he couldn't say out loud to Maggie had been built into the walls of her home instead. The awkward copper light fitting he had hung so carefully from the landing ceiling, the improvised front he'd made for the broken kitchen drawer. All of them a way of saying, *I am proud of you. I love you.* That is how Maggie had always seen it. His help, his daily presence in her life, was something physical and essential. She depended upon her father's ability to fix what was broken.

Maggie and Heron work through the next box of papers

in silence, scrapping far more than they save. They work and she sees not what it will be like to be without him, but what it will be like to wait. Maggie will live with this now, the anticipation of grief, for all the months and years it will take. The time before has already gone. The time when everything was simply fine. Her life, her work, her family. All of it ticking over. Now there would be this—life, but harder, then harder still. And in among it all, she feels a strange kind of relief, too. This is a day she has been waiting for all her life. Her chance to repay him. The one who loved her. The one who stayed.

Child protection

At the drive-through, Maggie agrees that a girl who won 2–0 in the morning and spent the afternoon dressed as a lion's mane jellyfish should indeed have large fries and a milkshake. Maggie says, "Yes, whatever you like," yes to everything. The day has been too long already, the thought of cooking dinner is simply laughable.

"Get a cheeseburger for me, and one for Dad, and whatever it is Tom likes."

Between mouthfuls of disappointing cheeseburger, Maggie and Conor catch up on the week just past. His client meeting: a success. Her new intern: off to a good start. Milly, or Tilly, or even quite possibly Lily. Tom and Olivia eat their fries and burgers. They make slurping plastic-scratching noises with their straws. The parents eat theirs and wait for the children to get lost in the TV. In lowered voices Maggie and Conor agree. They will keep it to themselves for now. It is too much for the children to cope with, reality. A grandad who is not invincible. Illness, death. All of it. That is what parents do; it is their job to protect children from painful truths.

Conor takes charge of the evening routine that night. Maggie needs more time to practice, to make sure it isn't written all over her face. He will check that Olivia has cleaned her teeth and fed the goldfish. He'll see to it that Tom switches off his phone, bore him with the usual reminder of the importance of sleep. These are the times when Maggie is most in love with her husband. The times when it would be strangest to say it. She loves him when he drives the car on long, dull stretches of motorway, keeping them all safe, taking them home. She loves him when he makes small talk at her work Christmas party, never seeming bored, even when talking to objectively boring people. It is not what she imagined when she sat on sofa beds with her teenage friends, VHS rom-coms and microwaved popcorn. This is real love, she is sure, practical and safe.

The evening follows a familiar rhythm. Maggie pulls Olivia's pajamas out of the dryer and shakes the creases from the solar system. She folds the pajamas first, always, because she finds them the most satisfying. Lining up the soft little trousers inside the top, just like they do in the shops, a cozy parcel to place on her daughter's pillow. She doesn't have time for grieving, or thinking in general; she has all this to do. All this work that is not her job. All the things she tells herself must be done to keep a family, a life, running smoothly. She doesn't know, exactly, when she turned into a woman like this. A woman who wonders, vaguely, and with no real desire to change, about whether the family should switch to oat milk. A woman who knows now that her father is dying but could not find the words to speak to him about it. Because in some ways she is embarrassed by her thoughts on the matter, by the things she would say if she said anything at all. She cannot say, you cannot die, not now, because I will sometimes want to call you, to tell you a joke I read in the paper, or that I saw a famous person on the platform at London Bridge. You cannot die, because you will be missing from the photographs of all the days that haven't happened yet—the children grown up, graduations, weddings, their babies. Maggie knows you cannot tell someone they are not permitted to die, no matter how reasonable the request.

And other stories

Maggie and Conor don't argue often, but they do argue about this, periodically, and in different genres. Sometimes it is a hushed and through-the-teeth discussion. More rarely they let loose, a real fight, conducted at volume, with tears and swearing.

Conor is pushing the topic again. He is just asking her, he says, to give it some thought. To consider the possibility.

"There are lost people everywhere," Maggie says. "Some people are just lost. You need to drop it." But Conor can't, or won't, understand what that means.

In the first week after he told her about the diagnosis, Heron and Maggie said no more about it. The time would come, they implicitly agreed, when it would become the only thing. Better for now, healthier even, Maggie told herself, to carry on as normal. Still, she starts to notice things she hadn't noticed before. The plastic trays of tablets in his bathroom drawer. His ongoing urge to sort out old paperwork, purging what isn't needed. Maggie didn't interfere. If that's what he wanted to do, she should let him. There would be plenty of time for sadness, they both knew that, but not now, not yet.

Conor is exhausted with the pair of them. Their silences. He thinks it is an opportunity. A turning point. "Surely it's the perfect time to talk to your dad about all that," he says. "There's so much you don't know about her; you should just ask."

"What is there to know, Conor?" Maggie fires back. "It's the last thing I'd talk to him about right now."

So Conor raises his hands, the cornered good guy in a Western. He backs out of the room. He has been married to Maggie long enough to know when to surrender.

They met, unimaginatively, at university. Conor, into student politics for the popularity not the policy. Maggie, prone to overworking but funny when she let herself be. When Conor thinks about it now, it seems a million years ago, not twenty. House parties, lectures, all the early passion possible in a single bed. Back then they had both tried to pretend that their families didn't exist, acting as if they had hatched fully formed, just in time for Freshers' Week. It couldn't last. Maggie's dad was always there, in the background, a safety net, or maybe a tether, keeping her from straying too far from home. In all the time they were dating, she never missed her Sunday night phone call home. Insisting, always, that her father wasn't keeping tabs on her, he just liked to keep in touch, that was all. He was always there at the end of the phone line. Always there, waiting in his Volvo to collect her at the end of term. Conor still remembers the two girls Maggie shared a house with, the way they would tease him about it. "You know her dad's the protective type?" as he stood in his boxer shorts, trying to excavate a couple of mugs from Maggie's kitchen sink. He had laughed, rinsed the mugs half-heartedly, and ignored them. Just the usual jokes at a new boyfriend's expense. But the more he got to know Maggie, the more he wondered about it. The plans so easily dropped whenever her dad needed her. It wasn't seriously weird, he told his own friends, not creepy exactly, but it was definitely too much. The fit of their relationship just one size too small. Softly stifling.

It took almost a year before Maggie deemed him worthy of a visit home. By then Conor had started to imagine Heron as some great hulk of a man, a cartoon shotgun in the boot of his car to protect his little girl from the big bad world. Finally, one empty Sunday in the summer term they'd taken the train down together to have lunch with him. Conor, hair freshly cut, a semi-ironed shirt, offered his best handshake to a man who turned out to be gentle to the point of mute most of the time. It wasn't that Heron was overprotective of his daughter, Conor saw then, it was something mutual, a sort of force field that had grown around the pair of them. A protective shell they'd built over the years. He is used to it now, the way Heron and Maggie watch but do not see each other. Maggie tells Conor she is so close to her father because they have been through something together, survived for all those years just the two of them. As if it is all inevitable; indisputably true.

Conor thinks a lot about the father he does and does not want to be. Not quite like his own dad who has settled on a short but very specific list of fatherly duties. Carving meat. Paying the bill in restaurants. Anything to do with cars. Not quite like Heron, either, who is far more hands-on but never, it seems to

Conor, entirely happy. For a long time Conor thought father-hood was all about doing things. When they had babies, Conor changed nappies, he pushed the pushchair. He did all the things he was supposed to do. As the children got older, he did all the next things too, homework and shoelaces and bad jokes. He'd had a DAD'S TAXI sticker in the back window of his car for years, until Tom had refused to get in again unless it was scraped off.

Sometimes, when he is alone with Olivia, Conor tries to imagine it, that parallel universe where it is just the two of them, father and daughter against the world. Just him to pick her up from school and make her dinner. Just him to help her find her lost library book or listen to whatever playground drama is currently at the center of her life. He thinks about the other side of it, too. Only her. Just a little girl to be the sounding board against all the weight of work and bills and disappoint-ment and loneliness.

Conor keeps a secret note on his phone called *Topics to talk to the children about*. He notes the names of their friends, the TV shows and computer games they adore and which he has never heard of. He writes it all down and then he talks. He asks. He listens.

Conor has to ask her again, he can't help himself, even though she has told him not to. He is sure Maggie will regret it, that they all will, so he brings it up as he is draining spaghetti over the sink, leaning back to keep the steam from fogging his glasses.

"Aren't you even curious, Maggie? She's probably still alive. Living in Spain or somewhere. She could have other kids."

Maggie feels it in her jaw, the ache of keeping her mouth closed with the effort of not screaming at her husband. For being so naive. For being so unremittingly thoughtful. It is so obvious to Maggie that it would be a betrayal to ask Heron about her mother now. She is astounded that Conor cannot see that. It would be unthinkable, to turn toward a stranger, just at the moment her father needs her most.

Somehow she breathes. Somehow she swallows the scream, and then she says, "She had an affair. They got divorced. She moved away. Fine. But whoever he was, she chose him over my dad. She chose him over me."

NOVEMBER 1982

The rules apply to everyone

After assembly, Hazel gives her class busywork and the children bend their heads over their desks in concentration. In the silence, she watches a seven-year-old boy pick at a scab on his left elbow. He makes a little trap door of it, opening and closing, until he finally picks it off, letting the scab fall on the navy carpet tiles. The new skin pink and fresh and shining.

She lets herself think about it. Earlier that morning, Dawn standing against the front door, pulling her in. One hand on the back of her neck, fingers threading through her hair as she kissed her. On the other side of the frosted glass life carried on. Children scuffing a ball off the curb. A dog barking in the flat downstairs. It was a kiss to lose time in. To lose all sense of place. And then Dawn had frozen, as if suddenly working something out. She had drawn back to look Hazel in the eye and said, "The parts of my life have played in the wrong order. I should have met you first."

Hazel had tried to cut her short, to lean her body against Dawn's and kiss her into silence.

"Really, though," Dawn had tried again, holding Hazel by

the shoulders, making her listen. "I wish I was the first person you loved."

"Who says you're not?"

This had made Dawn laugh at least, Hazel's too-charming response breaking the mood, letting some light in.

"And there's me imagining a long list of broken hearts behind you, all this time."

There have been others, Hazel admits, two she will tell Dawn all about when there is more time. One she would rather not go into. A couple more too fleeting to be worth raking up.

"And none of these is counting Jill," she says. Jill, who turns out to be just a girl from school, or Hazel's first true love, depending on how you want to look at it.

"Tell me," Dawn says, "please." She needs to know where she fits into Hazel's story. She needs to ask what might happen next, in hers.

Hazel protests, the time, she has to get to work. Until Dawn moves her arms around Hazel's waist, locks her fingers at the small of her back, and insists, she has five minutes, probably ten, and she gives in.

"My mother was worried," Hazel says. "She said Jill was a bad influence, a bit common. She found my diary."

"What happened?"

"She burned it. A bit dramatic, I thought. And we quarreled. You know the sort of thing. She said she was glad she had my brother. At least she had one normal child to make her happy."

Dawn isn't surprised, it is what she'd imagined, more or less.

"So what, you walked out?"

"We sort of came to an arrangement, so she could save face in front of the neighbors. They packed me off to teacher training college for a fresh start away from all the devil's temptations."

"I see." Dawn brings a hand up to Hazel's face, strokes a strand of stray hair behind her ear. "And how's that working out for you, Miss Wright?"

A laughing kiss. A holding tight. The beginnings of what the kiss might become, but time is there, filling up the narrow hallway of the flat, spoiling things. Hazel sighs, shakes the creases from her dress, picks up her keys from the hall table. The day is out there, waiting.

"I saw her, Jill, years later when I came home for the holidays. She was hanging nappies out to dry, the Silver Cross parked up by the back door, the whole business. She invited me in, but I said I was late for the train. We both knew it wasn't gone." Hazel shakes the thought away, that other life, long behind her. "And . . . ?" She looks back at Dawn now. "Your turn."

"Me? No. Not like this anyway."

"You always wanted to get married?"

"I think it's different for you," Dawn says. "College, your job. All of that. You can choose something else. The truth is he was nice, is nice. He took me to places. Not restaurants or anything. We took the ferry to the Isle of Wight once as foot passengers. I thought it was romantic. I'd never been anywhere. It made me exist, being someone's girlfriend, someone's wife."

"That's fair enough. You wanted to collect the set, the wedding, the house, the baby?"

Dawn shrugs her shoulders. "I didn't know you were allowed not to."

The more Hazel thinks about it the more certain she is. She is the only one who can make it all stop. If she leaves now, there's a chance Heron will drop it, let the whole thing pass by. If she can just disappear. Start again. In the way she usually does.

She stirs from her thoughts when the volume starts to rise, something is traveling around the classroom, the children whispering and nudging each other.

"Is it true, Miss? Is it true what they're all saying?"

Fiona Murphy, eyes like an owl, blinking behind her big round glasses, looks up and asks Hazel again, "Is it true?"

"Is what true?" She feels it in her chest, in the back of her throat. She knows what is coming: the accusation. Next it will be parents on the telephone. Explaining why she's not fit to be there. The headmistress, if she's lucky, letting her slip away quietly over the Christmas holidays with no more said about it.

"Is what true?" She steadies her voice. Tries to keep her face a blank page.

"Is it true," the owl girl asks, "that teachers make school pencils out of bees? Daniel J. says they put bees in one end of the machine, and black-and-yellow pencils come out the other end."

"No," Hazel says to her class, "that's not true," and a little disappointed sigh blows a soft breeze around the classroom. "But it is true that the red tips taste of strawberries."

Hazel picks up the chalk duster, turns her back to the class, as twenty-nine delighted children nibble the red paint from the ends of their pencils.

Later, the school day finished at last, Hazel closes her eyes. She breathes out. She goes the whole hog and puts her forehead on the desk and rests for a moment in the darkness of her sleeve. In the hour after the last bell rings, Hazel's head echoes with the sound of her own name. Miss Wright! Please, Miss! Hands up and voices high, calling for help or attention, hundreds of times a day. Now, she sits, in the first quiet moment of the day, and lets it fade down to silence. She lets the sounds of the children's voices clear. Seven sevens are forty-nine. Divorced, beheaded, died, divorced, beheaded, survived. She stands and wipes a diagram of the earth's core from the board; she opens the window and lets the chalk dust out in white clouds, in loud, soft smacks.

There is space to think in an empty classroom, the right kind of air. Hazel really did think it might be fine this time, or saw, at least, a flash of possibility. She knew someone who knew someone who had made it work, or maybe that was just a rumor. She thought things had changed, just enough. In truth, she thought their plan to tell him was sort of beautiful, romantic even, until it wasn't. Now it looked like something else, something reckless and naive. Hazel thinks; she tries to work out how to fix this. There were other options, surely. Bigger towns, where nobody would know them. Places where Dawn would be Hazel's lodger if it came to that, or Hazel would be hers. There were cities, wild little parts of London or Manchester where it was possible, surely, to be Mummy's Special Friend, to be a sort of family even. If they could get him to understand. To allow it. And if not?

On afternoons like this, when she is alone, Hazel tries to fall out of love with Dawn. She makes a list of all her bad habits, the way she leaves the lid off the butter dish, the way she sticks the old bits of soap together rather than starting a new bar. She thinks of all Dawn's imperfections, the strange bit on her left ear that's like an elf's, or a small rash she had once on her elbow, and she tries to be disgusted instead of charmed by them. Hazel tells herself lies. It's the only thing she can think to do. She tells herself she isn't hopelessly in love with Dawn. She tells herself she hasn't known it since the very first time she saw her. She tells herself she wouldn't do anything to have her. To save her from what is to come.

There is work to finish before she can leave the school. Spelling tests waiting for her red ticks, the stack of project books with their wide lines and wallpaper covers. Hazel is glad of the distraction, giving each book her close attention. The one with the pictures of cats, carefully cut out from magazines, then stuck back together again in a surreal collage of tails and eyes. Next, a particularly precise cross-section of a volcano, which deserves one of her gold stars. Hazel marks and she thinks. She doesn't know the man, only Dawn's version of him, and the things she can tell by looking at him. This man, who has always smiled at her politely, then looked straight through her. Just that woman his wife knows. Just that friend. For now it is contained, kept between the three of them, at least for as long as he wants it to be. But Hazel knows what happens next. Whispering at the school gates. Dawn's family ringing her doorbell with some less-than-gentle advice. People will appear from all corners now, ready to squeeze them back into their places or out of sight entirely. Hazel puts the children's chairs up on the desks to make life easier for the cleaner. She writes tomorrow's date in the corner of the blackboard and checks her desk is tidy, her classroom ready to start again. Tomorrow is coming, and all the days after it.

It takes so much
work to find them

So much work, and so much time. When Dawn first spots the advert in the back of the Sunday newspaper she thinks it is a miracle, or a trap. But it can hardly make things worse, she thinks, to send off for a magazine, so she does. Dawn writes a letter in her neatest handwriting, addressed to a PO Box in west London. The reply arrives a week later, an ember of hot-white hope landing on the doormat.

She finds what she is looking for in the magazine's classifieds, one square inch of words and a phone number. She makes the call from a telephone box behind the multistory car park, piss-smelling and cold. "Do you know it? The Arena Bookshop?" the woman asks her. "They let us use the room out the back. We take it in turns to bring the biscuits."

Dawn hangs up and stares at the note, scribbled on the inside cover of her address book—*Thursdays 8 p.m., Euston*—and wonders what on earth she will do with this information now that she has it.

//////////

It hadn't lasted, the truce between them that day in the park. "It is better, easier," Heron had started to say, if Dawn cut down on the time she spent with Maggie.

"Easier for who?" Dawn asks, but none of his answers are good ones. Heron changes plan, his mother suddenly helping, taking Maggie to playgroup, sitting with her until he finishes work.

"*I'm* her mother," Dawn roars at him, or she hisses. It doesn't make a difference. "I'm right *here*. I should be doing all of that. There's no reason I can't."

"It'll confuse her," Heron says. "It'll upset her to see you. This is easier. This is better."

When the letter arrives, the envelope makes them laugh— her name, Hazel's address. But the letter isn't funny at all, the long sentences and letterheads. Divorce, which seems fair, a relief even. But the rest of it. The rest of it eats her alive one bite at a time.

For weeks, for a month, in fact, Dawn does not go to the support group, but she does work out how. The train and two buses it will take. She walks the lines of unfamiliar streets with her fingers in the pages of her *Pocket A–Z*. Once, she goes all the way to the bookshop, at the wrong time and on the wrong day, a reconnaissance mission. She wants to see the street, to walk past the place where they meet, trying to sense them, an animal tracing its route back home.

She doesn't go in because she is afraid that the women will be strange, not like her. Or maybe worse, she is afraid that they will be just like her, that they will wear the same clothes and listen to the same music. She is afraid that she will be just like them.

She arrives in Euston to wet-leaf pavements, to the darkness of a November afternoon that might as well be night. She plays the role of a woman looking in a bookshop window, hands deep in pockets, chin tucked into the hiding place of her mohair scarf. If she is seen here, she will say she was just window-shopping. I thought it was just a bookshop. A normal bookshop.

The sign on the glass door panel is turned to CLOSED, but Dawn can see the light in the back room, yellow and glowing. The shapes of women, arranging chairs, passing mugs. Her reflection in the glass is strange, like a statue, like a ghost. She shakes her hair—this weather is a disaster for curls—she stands up straight. She has made an effort: best earrings, newish coat. Armor to keep her safe. Dawn watches the woman walk toward her through the darkness of the closed shop, turning the latch to open the door, letting in the air from the cold street. The woman, tall and smiling, who says, "Are you coming in?" before she leads Dawn gently by the elbow, past the shelves of other people's stories.

The room at the back of the bookshop is small, and the women sit knee to knee. The first time she joins them, Dawn does not speak. She nods her head and holds her herbal tea close to her face, letting the steam warm her cheeks. She tries not to stare at the two women sitting opposite, the quiet way they hold hands, the way they look at each other. The woman beside Dawn is wearing suede boots, dark green, baggy at the ankle, the perfect heel. Dawn has seen them in the window of Russell and Bromley. Her name is Sue, she has two sons. She only went to court, she tells the group, to get the children away from her husband, who turned out to be the type to hold your hand to the kitchen table and use your forearm as an ashtray.

The other women listen, they let her talk, and Dawn wants them to be more surprised. She wants someone to call the police, someone to do something, when Sue says, "His lawyers said we were dressing them up as girls. Putting ribbons in their hair. The judge didn't want to hear a word of what he'd done to me."

Dawn comes back to the group the next week and the next. She learns about the never-ending battles with social workers, the cost of solicitors' letters. She listens to the women who strike deals with husbands, the ones who find a way to make it work. The ones who don't.

In the gaps between, the women share other scraps of their lives. Melanie, whose son has got into the grammar school. Caroline, who has had her first driving lesson, after all these years. It is just like every other mother's group Dawn has been to. Tired women doing their best. When she listens to them, she can't understand why the courts bother, why all this effort is being used up on these ordinary women. At the end of one evening, Dawn finds Sue stacking up the chairs and asks the question that has bothered her all this time, "What harm are they doing to anyone?" Sue had smiled at her, paused to find the words to break it to this young woman, the world, and what it was really like. "They are terrified," she said to Dawn, "that's what it is. Think about how it looks to them. Mothers, housewives, shacking up together. We'd bring the whole system down."

A solicitor comes to the group one night, a serious woman in a dark blue suit.

"There's more chance of salvaging something," she says, "if you can prove to the court that you live alone. Persuade the judge it was a one-off, not a lifestyle." She admits an out-of-court settlement is usually safest. If you're willing to play the good girl, you might get as much as every other weekend and half the school holidays, say. If you can persuade your girlfriend to disappear at regular intervals. If you can get your husband to sign up to it, that is.

"And if he doesn't?" they ask.

On the bus home Dawn sits next to the window, folding her ticket into a tiny paper airplane. All the women in the support group have told her to avoid court if she can. If he's a reasonable man, they should try and come to a private arrangement. But it is already too late. The court date is set. Heron, naturally, wants to do it all by the book. Really, she thinks, he wants someone to blame for all this fuss. Deep down, Dawn knows, her story will be different. She's sorry for these other women, she really is, but she will explain it all, make it clear. Her love for her daughter is a kind of scientific truth, solid and measurable, anyone can see that. When the women in the group read aloud from their judgments, Dawn holds her breath as if warding off their bad luck. These judges who take it all so personally, standing as the last line of defense between innocent mothers and dangerous women who might seduce them in the supermarket. Nothing about being with Hazel feels like a bad influence to Dawn. It feels like electricity.

On brighter days Dawn knows that finding the group has helped, she knows now that she is not the only one. Still, it is a risk. "Don't tell anyone you've been here," Sue tells her. "Not even your solicitor. It will make you seem political. They don't like political." It wouldn't matter anyway. Heron has sent someone to follow her, or the solicitor has. She's seen a man, awkward and overdressed, some clerk from the office, probably, trying to look like a normal person. She's noticed him at bus stops and in the phone box near the flat. He must have watched her, surely, going into the bookshop each Thursday, and afterward, turning the key in Hazel's front door, pulling the curtains. Dawn's solicitor had warned her not to move in permanently. It might look, he had said, as if she had already made her choice. But where else did they think she could go? Her friends were Heron's friends; they didn't want to get involved. She'd tried to stand on her own two feet. When she went to fill in the forms to apply for a flat of her own, the man at the council told her to go back to her husband.

It had taken a few minutes to make sense of it, that day on the doorstep. Her key sliding into the lock as it always had, in, but not turning. Stiff and useless. Heron and Maggie weren't home, that much was clear. She'd looked through the window, and the letterbox, seen that Maggie's coat and welly boots were missing from their place in the porch. The side gate was high, but Dawn thought she might be able to climb it if she used the bin for a step up. And then what? A stone through the glass of the back door? Relying on the chance that the kitchen window had been left slightly ajar? The day was already starting, the street filling up with people who would have stopped to stare at a woman breaking into her own house. Dawn had looked around for help, or witnesses, and seen only teenagers in school uniforms, men in suits, walking in long strides to the station, a sandwich and a paperback tucked into their coat pockets. It would only add to the scandal if the neighbors saw her battering down the door. Dawn could already feel them watching her, waiting to see what she might do, from the safety of their semidetached lives. Dawn didn't huff or puff. Instead, she locked herself inside the car and made a list on the back cover of the road map of Great Britain: all the places she could go, all the people who would understand her. There was only Hazel's flat on the list. Only Hazel.

The journey back from the support group feels much longer than the journey there. Dawn walks from the bus stop and imagines herself, wills herself, already home. The flat will be warm, and Hazel will be there, standing at the hob, sipping at the edge of a wooden spoon to check if the dinner is ready. This is almost it, they say to each other, almost a life. They will get through this part, then they will live. They will need to find a bigger place of course, for the three of them. Space for Maggie's toys, her little bed.

Nobody is thinking of afterward

Heron tells Maggie that Mummy has gone on holiday, but Maggie sees Dawn watching her. Maggie sees her mother waiting for them in all the places they go. At the park, or across the street. Dawn follows them. She presses her face up against the window. Once, she screams through the letterbox like a madwoman. She begs.

"Please," she says over and over. "Please, Heron, she needs me."

It's all to the good, Heron's solicitor says. Evidence of instability. And he arranges a temporary order to be put in place, forbidding Dawn from seeing Maggie until after the hearing. Heron wonders if it's all a bit strong. A bit much. But what is he supposed to do? Act as if none of it matters?

By the end of November the solicitor's office has stopped feeling strange to Heron. It is routine now, the doorbell, the stairs, the bad coffee. The solicitor's voice, so familiar that he seems to hear it in his sleep, checking some detail on the paperwork, reassuring him that he's making the right decision. The only decision. When he is in the office, the weight of it is taken from him, handed over to people with the right letters after their names, the right kinds of cars. It's not an easy choice, he knows that, but it is the only one he can make, given the circumstances. Today they are going through statements, completing any final preparations. The solicitor moves pages from one folder to the next. He hovers the nib of his silver ballpoint pen just above the page, scanning the words, testing their impact.

"Your mother's on hand most days, that'll be half of it. The court is usually keen on some kind of female influence, for a girl."

"Right," Heron says. "I can see that."

"Anyone else on the scene we should know about? Girl-friend? Fiancée would be even better."

"No," Heron says, "no."

"Well, only a matter of time. Man of your age. Then it'll be fresh starts all round."

Dawn's solicitor tells her what to wear in court. Something a good mother would wear. A skirt. She takes the escalator up to the second floor of the department store and decides, as she cuts through haberdashery, that she will kidnap her daughter. It is the obvious thing to do. The garden of the playgroup might be easiest. She could turn up tomorrow morning and say there's been a change of plan, an almost forgotten checkup at the dentist. She could simply pick the child up and walk out with her. Except they've probably been warned, told to keep an eye out. Fine. She'll have to take Maggie from home, then. She'll watch for Heron's mother to arrive, wait for him to leave for work, then force her way in. Dawn will happily knock that hateful old woman to the floor if she has to. She will snatch Maggie up in her arms. She will drive to Dover and onto a boat that will take them far away from all of this. She buys a skirt and a blouse with a bow at the collar. They are clothes a mother would wear. Clothes his mother would wear.

DECEMBER 2022

It's hard, but when you're having fun

Maggie's daughter sits at the desk in her bedroom, writing a Christmas card for every child in her class. Her task will surely never be finished, since she plans to write a long and personalized message, in gold pen, to each recipient. When she remembers, Olivia dots each letter *i* with a heart. On a small selection she troubles herself to doodle a sprig of holly, or a careful snowflake. On even fewer, she seals the envelope with a foil Santa sticker, the code by which eight-year-old girls say, I am devoted to you.

Tom is in his bedroom, too, flat on his bed, eyes to the ceiling. He is supposed to be at his desk. It is Saturday morning, which means homework. Instead, he dozes. He dreams of a future without quadratic equations, a life where nobody will ask him to compare and contrast. Tom, doing little, thinking much. Waiting it out.

Downstairs, in the kitchen, Maggie opens her magazine on the counter in front of her, a prop to show the rest of them that she is busy and should not be disturbed. An hour earlier, as they were eating breakfast, Conor had called her "Saint Maggie, the Blessed Martyr of Christmas Planning," and she'd chipped one of her favorite coffee mugs, huffing it into the washing up bowl. Somebody should make that into a poster, she thinks, "Love is . . . someone telling you the truth about yourself before you've even finished breakfast." Or a snappier version of it anyway. Maggie has spent more of her life with this man than without him. All of her most important places and people stemmed from their togetherness, and yet, how easily she might have murdered him today rather than listen to the sound he made eating toast.

"I am only trying," she had said, "to make happy memories. For all of us."

In a tone of voice which even she could see was less festive homemaker, and more a person stoically holding it together through a bout of gastric flu. The little row is a sign she needs to get out of the house, reset the family's mood before the whole weekend turns sour. Maggie finds Conor on the driveway, hoovering the inside of his car, and heroically holds back any comment.

"I'm going to pop over and see Dad, just for half an hour." Her apology.

"I'll do lunch when you get back." His.

Heron keeps his Christmas tree alive all year, waiting in a glazed pot beside the shed, a pleasing concession to climate change. By rights, the tree should be quite impressive by now, but, much like its owner, it grows rounder rather than taller each year. The transfer from outdoor to indoor life complete, he leaves the tree standing on newspaper by the back door, acclimatizing, and heads upstairs to collect the decorations from the attic.

Heron thinks of the decorations box as a time capsule, everything just as he left it last year, and the year before that. Red tinsel and *Nutcracker* soldiers, various baubles, all dated but serviceable. Heron hangs the decorations carefully, heavier ones toward the center, lighter treasures made by Maggie, or, more recently, Tom and Olivia, on the outer branches. Pieces of precious paper that have somehow survived, gold cardboard robins with red glitter wings. Something which looks like a peacock but must be, what? A calling bird? A French hen? Heron stands back to admire the decorated tree. It'll do him good to have something heartening to look at in the evenings. A bit of festive spirit.

When the tree is finished he goes out to the garage, finds the nest of outdoor lights, and sets to work wrapping loops around the bay tree by the front gate. Most of the houses on his street have been decorated for weeks now. A full herd of neon reindeer gambol across the front lawn directly opposite. Farther down, a string of LED icicles drip from the garage roof. Next door has an inflatable snowman on their front doorstep. Each evening at six the snowman powers up, puffs out, glows. Heron quite likes the snowman, its friendly face. Maggie had been less complimentary about it, "leering" she'd said, and something about electricity bills. A string of lights is a fair contribution, Heron thinks, a show of willing. He needs the stepladder to reach the highest point, spreading the lights evenly about the tree. From the top of the ladder he sees his neighbor, David, from the bungalow on the corner, walking his pointlessly small dog. Always polite, Heron pauses his work and climbs down from the stepladder to chat. The weather is mild for December, David tells him, according to official records, and Heron agrees that it does seem that way. David asks Heron if he has seen the news about that politician, and Heron confirms that, yes, they do all seem to be at it nowadays. "Anyway," David says, nodding at the lights, "I suppose we've both seen more Christmases than we'll see again. Cheerio." And he leaves. A swift tug of the leash, the dog's stiff little legs a blur as it tries to keep up. Heron waves his neighbor goodbye, the miserable sod, and in one motion turns the same wave into a cheerful hello as Maggie's car pulls onto his drive.

"Perfect timing," he says, as Maggie locks her car with a click of the key fob, the wing mirrors folding in like some metal creature settling down to sleep. He will pack away the ladder and she can stick the kettle on. Maggie hangs her winter coat up in the porch, looks without looking at Heron's post on the hall table. A water bill. A circular from the estate agents. She takes the kettle to the kitchen tap, sees Heron has excavated more boxes from his loft and flicks through some papers as the water boils. A primary school project on mammals, the little white card that recorded her vaccinations—rubella: tick; measles: tick; mumps: tick. She unrolls a whole-school photo from 1991. Rows and rows of girls, shrunk to the size of Subbuteo players.

"Christ," she says aloud to the empty kitchen, as she stacks the mess into teetering piles, clearing space for their mugs. "It's breeding up there." It's irritating, actually, not endearing. All this dredging up of their past lives. She knows he thinks it is simply practical, but it feels morbid, all the frantic sorting out before he, they, run out of time. She can't face looking at the chaos, so she tips the lot into a sturdy tote bag so she can sort it out at home, one more box out of the way.

Over coffee they finalize the timings for Christmas Day, when Heron will arrive at hers, what he will bring. By the time she's buttoned up her coat, he is back in the garden doing something she doesn't understand with the compost heap.

"I'm off, then," Maggie calls from the back door, and Heron waves a goodbye with his trowel. There's no point in telling him that it's cold, that he should be resting, not digging. She waves back.

Maggie drives the long way home to make the most of it. The council's Christmas lights are up but not on at this time of the day. Candy canes, stockings, and the ones she knows are supposed to be baubles but look, undeniably, like spring onions. When she gets home she'll put the radio on, or a podcast. She'll sort through the latest bag of papers. Most if it will go in the recycling, but she's sure she'll find a few things to make the children laugh, an old passport immortalizing her teenage fringe, her *Smash Hits* autograph book.

Normality

At home, Maggie sits in the kitchen, flipping through the pages of the Christmas issue of *Home Trends*. She skips ahead to the main features and thinks about the other women reading this magazine in their kitchens right now. Other women, quietly oppressed by the concept of the Perfect Family Christmas, spending months preparing a tastefully aspirational table setting, or learning calligraphy for the sake of some handmade gift labels. Maggie judges these women, she thinks them shallow. Yet here she is, cutting out a recipe for clementine curd as if there were nothing more pressing to do with her time on this planet than sterilize a jam jar.

She can see how it might happen, how documents can be misfiled. She can imagine it. Envelopes easily slipped inside folders. Folders stacked into boxes. It's easy to see, when she thinks about it, how these three pages, held together with a single rusting staple, might find their way in among all the other pieces of forgotten paper. These few sheets of paper, just like any other. Just like the homework and the school reports. The thank-you notes and the ballet certificates. Just like all the documents with her name on them piled inside this box. All hers, one way or another.

Maggie reads the first page in one glance, whole, like swallowing food, too hot and too fast. The lump of new knowledge sticks in her throat. Burns her from the inside. She reads it again, slowly. It's a strange document, stern and official. A report about her, about all of them, but the family she reads about is not a family she recognizes. He has lied to her. She feels the weight of this settle, heavy and unfamiliar. He is still lying to her now.

That evening, her hair scraped back from her face, ready to work, Maggie wraps Christmas presents and makes a final list of the gifts she still needs to buy. The very specific lockable diary Olivia covets, in lilac not pink. Some generic bits and pieces for Tom—socks, maybe a book. There's a fantasy version of an evening like this, where Maggie wraps the children's gifts in front of a fire, an old movie—ideally black and white—playing in the background. Something mulled to sip. In practice, she sticks strips of tape to the edge of the coffee table to speed things up. She abandons ribbon and fancy labels, writing the children's names in the corner of each parcel with permanent marker pen. She watches an Australian baking show, the low-stakes drama soothing her, blocking out her new history, the revised version of who and how she is. She tries to tell herself she has misunderstood, jumped to conclusions that shouldn't be jumped to. Perhaps she has misread the report altogether. Or, she tells herself, she is overreacting, feeling too much because Christmas does that to people. It makes them sentimental. It makes them remember things.

////////

At the very end of her life, Maggie's grandmother turned back into a little girl, tucked into her favorite blankets, a small teddy bear held between her hands for comfort. For all of that last fortnight, Maggie spent each day after school sitting beside her, stroking her soft hair, lifting a beaker of orange squash for her to sip through a straw. Her mother's absence had already given Maggie a sort of glamour, almost, but not quite, a fairy-tale orphan. When her grandmother died, she became, just briefly, the most famous person in school. Wrapped in the comforting arms of older girls. The smell of coconut shampoo. Friends, and girls she hardly knew, gathering around her with hushed voices and mawkish hugs, as if her grief was contagious, had currency.

On the back of her Christmas present list, Maggie writes the names of all the women who helped Heron to raise her. Her grandmother, her teachers, her school friend's mum who explained to her about periods. A whole team of teenage babysitters and several well-meaning women of a certain age. They had all helped to take care of her in one way or another. They had all helped and they had all, presumably, known.

It's all for the children, really

On Christmas morning Tom ambles around the house, content. He eats the chocolate money he says he is too old for. He wears the novelty socks. He is satisfied with the offerings that have been placed before him. Earbuds, which his father says look like hearing aids. A pair of trainers, shocking both in size and cost. Still, his parents say, look, he is happy. We are all happy. It is different for Olivia, her reindeer slippers, all the new little plastic whatnots that need to be assembled and brought to life. All of it, the adults say, is for her, really. Olivia dashes from room to room, her joy already very close to something with tears. Maggie looks at the time on her phone, it is not yet eight in the morning.

They have all of the day's rituals still to get through, the performance of the dinner. Maggie finishes her coffee and murmurs her intent to go to the kitchen, to get the whole bloody thing started. It is, after all, all about the timing. Getting the turkey in on time to get the turkey out in time. The tricks she has picked up over the years; tenting the bird in foil to rest; her famous sprouts, which she will do, as always, with chestnuts and pancetta. The kitchen surfaces are cluttered with all the Christmas nonsense, jars of goose fat and all the other annual flourishes. She is grateful for the distraction of it, for the excuse to push everything else aside.

By midmorning they have a houseful. One of Conor's brothers, his wife, their baby. Conor's parents, who take up position on the smallest sofa, surveying their grandchildren as if the day, this whole life, is all their own handiwork. Heron arrives with the puddings, his contribution. As she cooks, Maggie listens, to the talking and laughing, someone always needing to know where the tiny Phillips screwdriver is. The new packet of batteries, lost again down the side of the sofa. All of it unrecognizable from her own childhood Christmases. It was bound to be different, a man and a little girl, making the best of it. Her cheeks tight from smiling all day to reassure him she was happy. It was television that came to the rescue. Each year Maggie would use a neon highlighter to mark up the big films and Christmas specials in the *Radio Times*. Little stepping stones of killed time they could both hop between: *Mary Poppins*, *Victoria Wood*, *Only Fools and Horses*. Familiar faces keeping her company in the long days before school started again. Sometimes, especially in the early years, the two of them would be invited to Christmas dinner at someone else's house. A gathering of waifs and strays, other families like theirs who had been cracked open by death or divorce. Maggie hated those Christmases, they weren't a distraction at all, but an underlining. Bringing all the spare people together made it even clearer who was missing.

Conor knows what to do on Christmas Day. He floats into the kitchen to wash up the odd pan. He pours the Buck's Fizz, a stagehand facilitating the main event. When he is called upon, Conor cuts toys free from plastic packaging, he reads the minuscule pamphlets for new gadgets as soon as he finds the instructions in English. He takes out the recycling before the piles of wrapping paper get out of hand. Conor knows that Christmas Day for Maggie is never about now and always about then.

Maggie shakes the potatoes in their hot fat, she prods at the turkey, and she remembers, against her will, all the unbidden things. Memories, let in by a smell or the color of someone's jumper. Here, from nowhere, a memory of the puppy Heron bought her for Christmas when she was nine. Maybe ten? Is that right? Not a gift, exactly, but some kind of implicit compensation for the lack of siblings.

"Some company," he had said.

Maggie remembers it perfectly, the months of preparation and buildup. Everything carefully picked out, the collar and leash, the bowl it would eat from. She remembers the lists of potential names written out in her careful cursive handwriting, weighing up the possibilities of Bouncer, Goldie, Honey, Kylie. The day the puppy arrived had been, she was sure, the happiest of her life. The chaos of the animal, pissing and chewing. The soft warmth of it, a toy come to life.

The puppy lived for a week.

"It can happen," the vet had told them. "Probably a weakness in the heart."

Afterward, Heron and Maggie walked home, taking their

own weak hearts with them. Nobody thought to replace the dog, so they carried on, just as before, without her.

It was a shock, seeing her mother's name, typed beside her own. Maggie realizes she has only ever seen it written down on official documents, her birth certificate, and now this. It is strange, eerie even, to hold written proof in her hands that Dawn Jacqueline Barnes (née Brown) really existed. Her mother is not in the family photograph albums. She is not in the archive of Heron's life anywhere, as far as Maggie can see. Her own recollections of her mother are, she knows, probably unreliable, mixed up with storybooks and a lifetime of encounters with other people's mothers. Wishful thinking in the place of real memories. She would like to have more concrete details to remember. She would, if she was really honest, like to know if they have anything in common. If there is something in the way she tucks her hair behind her ear when concentrating. If they both have the feeling of being at home when walking into a library. Her mother was, she thinks, a short woman. Can that be right? Surely she was too young to really remember anything? She was, Maggie is almost certain, a woman who made slightly too much spaghetti every time.

She must have asked about her at first. Where she was. When she was coming back. Maggie thinks of her own children at that age, how she couldn't go to the bathroom by herself without being followed. The way she was greeted like a returned hostage if she so much as went out for dinner with a friend. She must have asked and asked and asked about where her mother had gone. Then, she supposes, she must have stopped. She remembers how it bubbled under the surface again when she was about fourteen. All of her unasked questions taken out on poor Elaine. Elaine, twice divorced, with grown-up children and the one real girlfriend Maggie can remember Heron having. Maggie's response to a new woman in the house had been textbook: flouncing out of rooms, slamming doors, shouting the occasional insult as she went. Unimaginative but effective. She can't remember now, or never knew exactly, how it ended, but a furious teenage girl can hardly have helped.

When she idly threatened to run away at fifteen, to find her real mother, Heron had looked completely broken, so she stopped. Instead, she went through a phase of imagining her, making her up. Maggie invented a good mother for herself, witty, full of wise advice. She couldn't see then what was obvious now—Heron's loneliness is her fault. It's odd to think of this, unsettling, to see it all slotting into place. She must have been a burden to her father, still only in his twenties and left, literally, holding the baby.

When the Christmas dinner is served, everyone plays their part. They eat turkey and pull crackers and when someone elbows over a glass of shiraz, which soaks right through the tablecloth, nobody minds, because it is all unmatched chairs and passing the roast potatoes and asking who wants the last of the gravy. When they get to pudding, lit with a small blue flame, Olivia makes them all sing happy birthday to the baby Jesus, and the adults don't know whether to laugh or tell her off.

The kitchen recovers, the guests all taking a shift at the sink, and Maggie sits, finally, glass in hand, to open her gifts. Gifts that, she well knows, were purchased in some haste last weekend when Conor had finally taken the children into town and paid for whatever they picked out. From Tom, lavender bath oils, for which she is not ungrateful, even if it is a scent for old women or babies. He endures a hug of thanks as she coos over it.

"What a treat," she says. "I'll use it tonight."

Her son, so pleased with himself, the work of a minute, plucking it from the shelf. Then Olivia, at her side, beaming. Her gift is so well wrapped it is virtually laminated in Sellotape, but Maggie manages to tear at one corner and open it. Inside the parcel, she finds a small plastic box in the shape of Hello Kitty's head. Inside that, a pencil sharpener and matching rubber, a miniature set of glitter pens, and a tiny notepad.

"It's for your office. You can take it to work," her daughter says, and Maggie thanks her, tells her it is exactly what she needs.

In the late afternoon, people drift around the house looking for the next thing to do. The inevitable game of Monopoly starts up, some of the players genuinely willing, others less so. Someone suggests, as they must, a walk, to blow away the cobwebs. The idea sets everyone off on the hunt for shoes and coats. Maggie cuts the label from her new scarf, a gift from Conor, and loops it around her neck. A mossy green mohair, not a color she would have chosen for herself, but she likes it, it reminds her of something. The hallway is hot and crowded as the walkers gather, zipping and buttoning up, the baby is tucked into its fleece cocoon. It is dark now, and Conor plots a route along the nicest streets, showing off the big houses, their strings of white lights, real trees glowing golden in bay windows, as if they are accessories to his own life.

And all day long, she keeps it in. Maggie sets out plates and does not throw them at the wall. She carves and serves and slices and does not brandish any cutlery with intent. She keeps it in. There should have been screaming, she thinks. In other families there would be tears and raised voices and neighbors wondering if they should call someone or do something.

By the evening there is nowhere to hide. The whole family sits together, admiring the success of the day. Maggie looks at her father, his little plate of Christmas buffet, a tiny sherry glass in his hand, which makes him look like a giant. Olivia at his feet, carefully unpacking and repacking a set of heart-shaped nail varnishes. Maggie knows she could stand up and say it, interrupt the discussion about whether or not they should light the fire, just for the atmosphere. She could howl, I am sad beyond all normal sadness. Some essential part of me has crumbled in on itself. All of this, this day, this happiness, all of it is false. But she doesn't say any of it. She knows him. You were only a child, I was protecting you, he would say. I was trying my best. Maggie eats three kinds of cheese and does not say any of the words that would blow Christmas into glass shards. She cannot bring herself to spoil it. Maggie has not confronted Heron because she cannot imagine where to begin or how to end. All the impossible things she would need to say. He is ill, she thinks, he is fading out.

Heron, tired, full, sees his daughter looking at him and reads on her face a look of pity. That is my daughter observing me at Christmas, he thinks. Looking at me as if trying to store me up. Making me into a memory, in case it is the last. He had felt something similar earlier, when Conor had swept his phone around the table, filming them all in their paper hat grins. When they watched the video back, he saw himself, a figure in the background, the expression on his face doubtless wrong. His body held too upright, unmoving, while the people around him smiled, stretched out their arms to wave at the camera. There is talk of a game, charades maybe, or the drawing one. Heron surrenders, says he'll head up to bed. Nobody is in any fit state to drive the ten minutes back to his house. He would have walked, but Maggie insists. He should stay.

At the end of the spare bed Maggie has set out a folded towel, some miniature toiletries pinched from a hotel bathroom. All the thoughtful details that remind Heron he is not at home. The room is like a set from one of Maggie's magazines. The walls exactly the right shade of white. Soft lighting. Good linen. It is the first moment of quiet he can recall since arriving this morning. Heron opens the packet of new pajamas, a variation on the pajamas he has received for Christmas every year for as long as he can remember. When he lifts the towel he sees the brown envelope, and inside it, three sheets of paper, held together by a rusty staple.

The good glasses are still on the table, Conor swills two out under the cold tap and pours Maggie a full glass of red. She sits on the corner of the sofa, her feet tucked under her, hands heavy after the work of the day. She is relieved that her father has gone up to bed. He will find the court welfare report now; he will read it and think about what to say to her and when. She can settle into this new knowledge about herself. She can wait. Conor sits in the chair nearest the fire, fiddling with one of Olivia's new dolls, already short a limb. She watches her husband, his care and concentration as he struggles to plug plastic arm into plastic shoulder joint. She has a sip of her wine, takes a deep breath, and tells Conor what she knows. What she thinks she will and won't do next. Conor listens. He nods. He is not, he admits, sure of the right thing to say. All of this is bigger, stranger, than he thought it would be. When the doll's arm is fixed, he goes to the kitchen and opens the back door, releasing the fumes of goose fat and grieving out into the night sky.

DECEMBER 1982

Without fear or favor, affection or ill will

The courtroom is modern, everything in shining pale wood, as if fitted wardrobes have been left to grow wild. Dawn looks at Heron and does not know him. It seems laughable that they have ended up here. Impossible, that they would face each other in court, humiliate each other in front of strangers like this. She is annoyed to see he is wearing his C&A suit, his second-best.

It would be boring, all the procedure of it, the standing up and down, if it weren't for the fear collecting at the back of her throat, making her feel full up, too liquid. As if she might laugh, as if she might vomit. To start with, there are details to establish, a list of dates and facts lined up for inspection. There will be reports by qualified people, people who know what they are talking about. These are the processes of the Court. The lawyers will set the scene, then they will proceed. They will ask her, these lawyers, to defend herself or deny herself. People are expecting an explanation.

When their names are read aloud, Dawn realizes she hasn't heard him called Henry since their wedding day. She sits quietly as she has been told to do. Her unreasonable behavior will be spelled out for her. Her unsuitability. She feels too young to get through it all. She feels far too old.

Heron's barrister is a man who likes to introduce himself with a little joke. Usually he says, "James Paul. I know, two first names, isn't it an unbelievable mess?" Sometimes, if the occasion suits, he'll say, "The name's Paul, James Paul." This morning he had greeted Heron with an Oxbridge handshake and said, simply, "James Paul, we spoke on the telephone. Let's get this tidied up, Mr. Barnes, shall we?"

When Mr. James Paul stands to speak, Dawn knows she will remember this man's shoes for the rest of her life, his dainty little loafers, the type with the slight puckering around the front edge, a gold bar across the front. Whatever happens, she thinks, I will be haunted by this man and his delicate slip-on shoes.

They call the social worker first, houndstooth jacket sloping from his shoulders. It is his view, he says, then, correcting himself, it is his *professional* opinion that they are discussing a child at risk. Dawn lets out a noise at these words, a sound of deep surprise that escapes her against her will. The court politely ignores her, and the barrister presses for clarification.

"You mean to say you think Mrs. Barnes will harm her own daughter?"

"Not physically, perhaps," the social worker says. "But morally. This is a moral question."

Heron has never been in a courtroom before. It is not, it turns out, the same as on TV. He looks around at all the officials, their legal fees and Latin phrases, and sees that he has not lived the kind of life that would have prepared him for a day like this. Heron leans his arms on the table and sees that things are expected of him here. A deep sort of confidence. The moral high ground. He has never thought of himself as a bold man, certainly not a vengeful one. He just likes rules, that is all. When he was at school the other boys would make fun of him, the only one never to have seen the inside of the headmaster's study. Heron was a good boy, and now he is a good man. He believes this. He does not drive too fast. As a rule, he doesn't use bad language, at least not the really strong stuff, and certainly not in front of women. But he can see today where his goodness has got him.

Deferring to men who know which fork to use. Depending on the advice of men who wear cuff links. The lawyers have shown him the evidence, the shame of it would ruin Maggie's life. Having one of them as a mother would turn her the same way, the solicitor had said. They've explained to him that this is the best course of action, this is the only thing he can do. Pull them apart. Start again, just the two of them. Heron looks at all the people working to solve his problems and trusts that they know what to do. He feels he cannot stop it now, the case, and what will be left of them all afterward is out of his reach.

When the court adjourns for lunch, Heron buys an egg sandwich from the bakery across the street and warms his hands on a polystyrene teacup. It is far too cold to sit outside, but Heron isn't sure where he's supposed to go, or what he's allowed to do. His counsel are a few steps behind, catching up to join him, blowing on hands and stamping feet to keep warm. The solicitor, smoking as much as he is able in the time allowed. The barrister, sweeping his wool coat beneath him and saying, "We must," then softening, "we *should* consider turning up the volume this afternoon, don't you think?"

Heron feels the cold of the concrete bench seeping through his cheap raincoat, through his suit trousers. Cold that is also wet, leeching through at the backs of his knees. A thought comes then, an idea he can't account for. That if only he had the chance to sit there long enough, the cold might flow right into him, freeze him into clear, unthinking ice.

He chews quietly, there is tomato in the sandwich and it makes the bread too soggy. Ordinarily, he would take the tomato out, wrap it in the greaseproof paper bag, but he doesn't want the barrister to think he is fussy, childish.

"If we keep going as we are, softly-softly," the solicitor joins in, "the court will suggest a compromise. Shared custody, every other weekend and school holidays for Daddy, say. That is, essentially, a win for her."

They've already been through this. Heron has paid the steep hourly rate to hear their winning strategy spelled out in the clearest of terms across the solicitor's desk. But it is here, on this bench, the chill of the concrete working its way into his bones that Heron has a final chance to change course. He should move. Stand up. He should say something, slow them down at least. Because he does feel then as if he might say, yes, let's offer that. Doesn't that seem a fair way to manage this? People get divorced all the time. His daughter loves her mother. Couldn't he be a dad who takes his daughter bowling at the weekend? He could learn to like cheeseburgers. And then again, he cannot bear the thought of it, the years ahead stretching out, doorstep skirmishes over who will be alone on Christmas Day. He cannot face a lifetime of seeing the way Dawn looks at him now. As if he is the one who has changed, become unrecognizable. And really it is the other thing, the real problem he can't find another way to solve. How can he do that to his daughter? They've all been perfectly clear with him, the social worker, the lawyers. It is his duty, they've told him, to protect her, to save her from the strangeness of that life and what it might do to her. It's up to him to keep her safe from playground bullies. Worse things. From the risk of it all. Heron nods his head, he stays frozen to the bench, and he says yes.

"Yes, okay. Do what you need to do."

Not the answers,
but the questions

There is a little trick he has learned over the years, which helps. The whole time he questions her, Heron's barrister directs his gaze at Dawn's left earring, a tasteful little knot of gold. It helps him, not to look into the eyes of the person he is questioning. He is not distracted this way, by her shock, or whatever else passes across her face.

James Paul opens the folder on his desk and brings out the list of questions he knows will catch the judge's ear.

"Mrs. Barnes," he begins, "will you please explain a practical matter to the court?"

Dawn nods.

"When you and your lover have—" And here he pauses, makes quote marks in the air with his bent fingers around "sex." "What appliances do you use?"

Dawn blushes at the question and she does not understand it.

"Appliances?"

He goes on.

"Do you, Mrs. Barnes, make love in front of your child?

Do you make a noise when you have sex with that woman? Has your child heard you?"

When Dawn looks at her lap, at her hands clinging to each other and says, "What do you mean?" or "Of course not," Mr. James Paul simply fires another question, and another.

"Kissing, then, or holding hands. Has that little girl seen her mother kiss another woman on the lips?"

"You must answer, Mrs. Barnes," the judge says. "You must answer."

After the first set of questions Dawn keeps her head up; she tries to. The worst of it, surely, is over now. Tonight, she will try to explain to Hazel, describe it all. It was like a bad dream, she will say, where you have to sit for a really hard exam but you've only got a piece of string instead of a pen. That's what it's like. Unfair. Surreal. There is a short pause as Heron's barrister gathers some papers and Dawn thinks it will be her turn now, her chance to explain.

It is impossibly odd, seeing Hazel's letters, here, in his hands. Of all that has happened in the court already, it is this that hits her in the chest, a jolt of shock. How did he find them? Heron, to her knowledge, had never so much as opened the linen closet door. It had always been as if all the domestic nooks and crannies of their house were invisible to him. Did he turn the place upside down once she had gone, searching for evidence of her depravity? She can't imagine it. She catches his eye then, sees they are sharing the same thought. Of course. Not Heron, but his mother, opening the closet to put away Dawn's freshly washed sheets. Reaching up to bring out a warm towel for Maggie's bath.

"Those are private," Dawn says, but nothing is private now.

The judge agrees they can be read aloud for the benefit of the court. Read and copied down by the tap tap tap of the stenographer.

Her letters.

Dawn had always written to Hazel on the cream pages of her Basildon Bond writing set, kept for special occasions. Hazel's replies came on onionskin airmail paper, Par Avion envelopes, a joke between them she can't seem to remember now. Letters Dawn had held to her chest like a teenager, committing each word to memory. Nicknames and lines of poetry. Lyrics from songs they had made their own. They never posted them, of course, just passed them hand to hand. Sometimes Dawn would leave a letter for Hazel to find before she let herself out. Tucking the envelope behind a milk bottle in the fridge or under her pillow for her to find before bed.

The barrister waves a handful of pale blue pages above his head, and she can see the lazy tails of Hazel's handwriting from where she is sitting. The y's in her "whys" falling off the line above. She can hardly deny they are real.

"We must get away, just for a day." His voice curdles Hazel's words. "We'll hold hands and eat a picnic lunch on the beach. Or buy chips? Did you ever go to Cromer as a child?"

The barrister reads their dreams aloud, the dinners in restaurants they might have, white tablecloths and candles. Hotel rooms in far-off cities. A little house of their own with their things displayed on the shelves. It is like something from an old novel, Dawn thinks. Romantic and harmless. All their unambitious little fantasies. All the clichés they had saved up from Hollywood movies and teenage crushes.

"You are planning to abandon your child, Mrs. Barnes?"

Here is the evidence, he says, written in Biro, a house by the sea.

"Not a plan," Dawn insists, "just a game. Or a joke."

"You think leaving your husband and child is a joke?"

"No," she says, "of course not. I mean, you're misunderstanding the letters, what they are about."

"Am I?" His slow, careful voice a cassette tape about to warp and snap. "Am I, Mrs. Barnes? It all seems pretty clear to me."

There is so little lust to find in the letters. They weren't fools. Is this what they are accusing her of, Dawn wonders, the dream of swapping one kitchen sink for another? Still, he finds enough, or something that will do, anyway. The barrister raises his eyebrows, scans the room, and Hazel's words rust as he reads.

"Just before I fall asleep, I kiss the inside of my left wrist, on the hidden place beneath my watch, just where you always kiss it. I'm sure there must be some trace of your lips that stays there. Will you pay in some deposits when I see you on Wednesday? I need you to leave one hundred kisses on my wrist so I can cash them in when we're apart."

Her understanding grows in layers, like sediment building up, compressing her into the deep core of the earth. There is no way of talking herself out of it, they are taking the letters as facts, as firm intentions. Nobody here can understand that it was only a safety valve, words written as a way to talk to each other when they couldn't meet or call. The whole point of the letters was that they were never real. A few lines in which they could write a life free of obstacles and consequences. They imagined another world was possible. It didn't mean they believed it was.

Dawn is furious at herself for letting this happen. She could have burned Hazel's letters so easily, or torn them into shreds. She could have soaked them to mush at the kitchen sink. She could have, at least, made this part harder for them. Her humiliation is, she understands, the whole point. But there is something else, too, the barrister's curiosity, the judge's appetite for more detail. They are afraid of her, of some power she has no idea how to wield.

There is nothing Dawn can say or do or cry about to change anyone's mind. It had seemed so obvious when she left the house that morning. She loved her daughter; that was the main thing. People would be reasonable. They would be fair. Now the barrister reads her private letters, and Dawn sits and thinks of all the ways she could have, should have, made these words disappear. Bleach. Fire. Scissors.

More experts are called to explain to Dawn the difference between right and wrong. The psychiatrist, who does not appear in person but sends his typed expertise to be read aloud to the judge. He has learned, this invisible man, over a lifetime of studying the children of prostitutes, that harm is inevitable in a case like this. Drugs. Crime. The usual. Dawn's barrister coughs, begs His Honor's pardon, but wonders if perhaps this evidence is quite appropriate here. "Something of a different situation, wouldn't you say?"

But His Honor would not say. He dismisses the challenge as if annoyed to have his concentration interrupted. This deviation from the natural way of things is much the same as that deviation, as far as he's concerned. It is permissible. So the report is read; the steady, certain voice of James Paul explaining to the court what becomes of children with perverts for mothers.

Two miles away from the county court building, Maggie holds her grandmother's hand. She points to the iced bun in the bakery window, the special one with red and white icing. Maggie has had lots of cakes recently. She has had toys, too, even though it isn't Christmas yet. A little plastic turtle that swims in the bath. A blue scooter with ribbons in the handlebars. When she asks for a lollipop now, she almost always gets one. Maggie is learning new lessons, about what you can and cannot ask. She sits with her grandmother at a table by the window and eats the whole iced bun, then licks her sticky fingers one by one. She asks if she can have another. Then she asks, again, when her mummy will be home.

Dawn thinks a lot about her face, what her body might be saying. She tries not to fold her arms. She tries not to frown. She tries not to smile, either. She doesn't know what combination of arms and eyes and mouth will keep her from looking ashamed. But she cannot look too brazen, either, too indifferent to it all. When she places her hands on the table, pressing down to stop the shaking, she has to stop herself from knocking on the desk, demanding the right to list the infinite number of things that only she knows about her little girl. She wants to tell them that she knows the scent of her daughter's skin, the exact curve of her fingernails. Dawn would like to explain to the court that Maggie only likes her toast cut into four small triangles, and that she calls them "cat ears." That her daughter keeps a pound note and a few copper coins in a pencil tin under her bed because she is saving up to buy a doll's house with real electric lights. Dawn wants to tell these men that she has loved that little girl since she was a girl herself, as if her own childhood dreams had conjured her into being. She cannot understand why they don't ask her any of this.

Instead, they ask about the sex. The when and how and who does what. The lawyers and the judge, who do not seem at all embarrassed, but rather treat this matter as essential evidence. Her discomfort, after all, is a self-inflicted wound. When James Paul asks her how many times she has made love to Hazel, she is tempted to laugh at the question, as if she kept a notebook, tallying off each time, awarding marks out of ten for effort. Dawn understands that any number is enough for his purposes. Enough to have transformed her beyond repair, enough to make it seem her sole occupation and obsession. This was the picture he was painting now, her selfish desire too great to be contained. No real mother would have risked it. No real mother would have wanted it. Dawn is lost to all the things that matter in this world.

That evening, Dawn insists she isn't hungry, but Hazel says she must try, just something small, to keep her strength up. Hazel searches the kitchen for anything that might tempt her and finds the postcard tucked beside the kettle. "Love is . . . living in hope," printed across the top; and underneath, a little cartoon boy on a desert island, a message in a bottle floating toward him. Hazel had bought one for Dawn, too, "Love is . . . when destiny calls," the little cartoon boy holding a bunch of flowers behind his back, while the little cartoon girl waits coyly behind the door as he rings the bell. More paper gestures. All their attempts to explain something to each other. In the card shop, the woman had grinned at them as they placed the cards side by side on the counter. Winked.

"Your boyfriends are lucky chaps," she'd said, and they had nearly died laughing, trying to pay.

Hazel sets a mug of tea on the tray, the last mince pie, something sweet against the shock of the day. The shame of the letters being read aloud. The questions Dawn will hear in her head for the rest of her life. She puts the mug in Dawn's hand, sits beside her, and she lies. "Everything will work itself out in the end," Hazel says.

It was only a few months ago that they'd bought the postcards. In a time before, when all of this was fun. It would be easiest to explain things in a note, Hazel thinks, as she watches Dawn sip her tea. The cowardly thing, but the easiest. She could write it all out carefully, her reasons, her hopes that this might solve it all, then she could lean the envelope beside the kettle for Dawn to find in the morning. There would be space in a letter for Hazel to explain that maybe, in the end, love is forcing yourself to leave.

JANUARY 2023

Antibodies defend, and they fight

Maggie flips her pillow onto the cool side, draws the duvet up to her chin. She has carried on as best she could, the fizzing vitamin C tablets, the steaming baths. In the last hour or so, she has started to float the idea that her cold is actually the flu.

From her hiding place in bed she listens to her family, marveling at how long it takes them to complete the simple task of leaving the house. Olivia's footsteps, smacking against the hall tiles as she runs back and forth in search of some small but essential talisman, a hair clip or a lip balm to stuff in her pocket. Tom mumbling, impatient now. If he's being dragged out, he wants to get going. He zips up his new coat, designed to protect its wearer against a Canadian winter. "I suppose it'll get you through a mild January in Kent, then?" Conor says, and Tom rolls his eyes, digs his hands deep into his fleece-lined pockets. When the door finally shuts behind them, a silence fills the house, different air flowing up the stairs and through each room. Maggie can hear herself now, the sound of the duvet as she rolls over. Outside, the neighbor's car reversing out of the drive. She closes her eyes and lets

Saturday morning stretch out ahead of her, listing off all the compensations of being mildly ill. The rest of them should be out until lunchtime; that's at least three hours of unwitnessed life. She contemplates a transfer from bed to sofa. She could watch some trashy television. She could, she hardly dares imagine it, read a book. There's nothing stopping her, strictly speaking, from picking up one of the many unread books she stockpiles in the hope of a day like this. In the end, Maggie chooses the most subversive option of all, she stays in bed. She lets the world and its responsibilities carry on beyond her bedroom curtains.

Later, when Conor walks into their bedroom, a mug in one hand, a small plate of tempting things to eat in the other, Maggie pretends she is still asleep. He sets the plate down on the bedside table, almonds, a green apple, the last of the sheep's milk cheese left over from Christmas, cut into little cubes, and waits for her to admit she is awake.

"The walk was fine," he tells her. "When the moaning got too much, I took them to that new café and let them order fancy hot chocolates, which by the way, turned out to be ten quid jam jars of liquid sugar topped with marshmallows."

Conor stops talking, runs his hand along the side of her face. It is a surprising touch, the kind they don't have time for anymore. A touch from a life when Saturday mornings still existed. When she would lie in bed, her back turned to him, as he wrote messages with his fingertips along the curve of her spine for her to decode, letter by letter.

"Are you feeling any better?"

"I don't know," she says. "A bit, I think. Maybe I'll have a shower, try to shake it off."

"Maybe you should just call your dad?" Conor says.

It is in the room then, more truth she does not want to hear.

"Why would I do that? What do you even mean?"

It is cheap, unconvincing, her attempt to make Conor the problem, and he is wise to it. Her husband, sitting on the edge of their bed, readjusting his pose, and turning to her as if she is a child, sulking because the bedtime story has finished too soon. Conor, who swallows the temptation to say to his wife, you are not ill, you are just sad. Conor, who chooses instead to say, "Perhaps it would do you both good."

In the shower, Maggie squeezes shampoo into the palm of her hand and thinks of all that is already lost. Her own childhood is so far away now, was it even worth it, going back in time like this? She rubs the shampoo into her scalp and thinks about the way children change, how quickly they become themselves. Maybe she can even understand it. The logic of saying nothing, of waiting for her to move past it all. Was that Heron's plan, just waiting for her to grow up into a person who didn't miss her mother? Maybe it was easy enough in the end. Maggie tries to remember if it was two or three years ago, when her daughter was still in love with her in that unrelenting way? Clinging to her when she walked into the room, leaving tiny handwritten notes under her pillow. That is the sort of love Olivia gives to her friends now, blind and intense. It changes almost by the day. Olivia has started to doubt her, Maggie

knows that. She has started to notice her mistakes, her imperfections. That's right, Maggie thinks, that's how it should be.
Mothers and daughters are real people, too. Olivia will need
to learn that. It had been different when she was younger, their
bond undiluted and possessive. Maggie remembers that phase,
when Olivia's love for her was a kind of jealousy, when she
had wanted all of Maggie to herself.

"It's not division," she had tried to explain to her daughter,
"it's multiplication. I don't love you any less because I love
Daddy and Tom too."

Her little girl had looked at her carefully and nodded.

"Or maybe you're a bee," Olivia had said. "A bee has three
hearts."

Maggie had looked it up that evening, and it was true to
a point, three hearts, or whatever system of valves and tubes
pass for a heart in bees. The vital system that keeps them going.

It is impossible, all this change. It is entirely inevitable.
Maggie presses her head with her fingertips, washing out her
thoughts, rinsing her brain clean. She turns the shower tem-
perature up too high, a slight but well-deserved scalding. She
is a grown woman; she cannot hide from her own life. Maggie
switches off the shower and stands in front of the bathroom
mirror, dotting face cream under her eyes and along her jawline, a constellation across her brow. Lately Maggie has started
to watch older women, admiring them, the way they live in
the world without being pinned down by it. The clothes they
choose. The way they speak to strangers. She looks at her reflection and has no idea if she has turned into her mother.

That is how it is, with timing

On the last day of the Christmas holidays, Maggie tells the children that their grandfather is ill. She sits them down, side by side on the sofa, as if they are kids in an American movie. She looks them in the eyes and she explains. When they both start to cry, she is unexpectedly furious. He is my father, not yours, she wants to scream at them. I am the person who is allowed to feel this. Her own children, with their soft, wet faces, rubbing knuckles in their eyes. She watches the news change them. Tom, nodding, saying nothing much at all. Olivia full of the questions an eight-year-old needs to ask, straightforward and uncensored.

"How quickly will he die?"

"Will we go to the funeral?"

"What will we have to wear?"

"All of that is a way off," Maggie says. "For now, we carry on. Go and feed the hamster. Go and do your homework."

Go and keep going.

She knows straightaway that she's made a hash of it. She has hurried them, rushed them through the bad news because she doesn't know another way to do it. She should have made this moment more bearable, set out sandbags of maternal comfort to keep the grief at bay. Instead, it is just another distancing, another moment she hasn't managed to get quite right. That is what the children will remember, Maggie thinks. On the day my mother told us our grandfather was dying, they will say, she made us pack away our emotions so she wouldn't have to look at them. They will have to add it to the list. One more wound for retelling in therapy, she supposed, or to a new lover in a soul-baring midnight conversation. That was my childhood, they will say. That was my mother. Cold.

Quite often now, Maggie thinks about what she will do when she receives the news of her own dying. There'll be a lump, say, or a pain that doesn't, in the end, turn out to be nothing. If she gets the news, that is. There's some good fortune in getting an advanced warning like that, in being given the information that you must live now while you can. Did her father know, before he went to the doctors? Our bodies tell us things. That was what it was like each time she was pregnant; her body told her before any test. Maggie thought it was an old wives' tale until it happened to her. Dying would be the same, she was sure. Her body would tell her. Maggie hopes that when it happens, she will live wildly, do something bold. She might get an unlikely tattoo or learn to skydive. Make the most of every last minute. But somewhere deep inside her, Maggie knows that she will not do anything of the sort. She suspects she will fail at her final living. She will keep on paying bills and tidying cupboards until it is unseemly, and then she will disappear. She will be too afraid, even then, to shake off her responsibilities.

To live freely. When the children were small, she would wake in the night with the fear of a sudden death, a vision of herself run down by a bus and nobody knowing where the nit comb was kept. She must live, she had told herself in those days, because she was needed. She must stay.

From the kitchen, the sound of talk radio turned up high, of pans being thrown on the hob with a flourish. The soundtrack of Conor making an extravagant brunch when the rest of the family would be happy with cereal. It was one of his tried-and-tested tactics, attempting to cheer Maggie up by cooking his favorite meal. She will go toward him. She will make the coffee. Maggie collects the cups, and as she starts to steam the milk, Olivia appears at the door, reindeer slippers on the wrong feet, her face all questions.

"Does it hurt Grandad, the cancer?" she asks, her eyes fixed on her parents. "Can't the doctors help him feel better? Can't they give him medicine?" Conor lifts his daughter up onto a kitchen stool and lets the poached eggs mind themselves for a minute. He holds her face in his hands.

"They will help. The doctors will help him. But bodies don't work forever."

Olivia looks at him steadily.

"Even mine?"

The four of them, at the kitchen table, on best behavior. Together. Even Tom is subdued into good manners by the bad news. They eat and they talk about their normal lives, which will start again tomorrow. School and work and all the people they

184 / CLAIRE LYNCH

must turn back into when they step outside this house. Maggie thinks about taking a photo but doesn't. When she looks at them like this she is always surprised, this perfect family. She cannot remember now if she imagined being a mother when she was a little girl, but she could not, surely, have imagined anything like this. The oddness of being in love with people who become less and less known to you each year. When she reaches across the table for the milk jug, she feels a lip of flesh flop over her waistband. It is a release. An undeniable truth.

When the food is all gone, they disperse around the house. Each of them in search of something to do, something real to touch. Tom, thumbs on the Xbox controller, sets his footballers to run and run. Olivia threads beads to make her complicated knots of friendship. Conor takes down the last of the Christmas lights still pinned around the front door. The end of all of that for another year. Maggie lowers the cast-iron pan into the sink. The children have understood something new today—nothing changes, everything does. She dries her hands on the tea towel, rotates through the usual apps on her phone, looking and looking for something she can't find. She is an adult. She feels certain about nothing. She is a woman who always reads the label. She has hair that never looks quite how she wants it to anymore—not awful exactly, just not right. She will go and see her father.

A game of chess

Maggie rings the doorbell and Heron understands what that means. She has moved toward him, but only one square. This is not a reconciliation, not yet.

She is ready for him, full of words and fury and questions. When he opens the door she will roar, let it all fly at him.

But the words that come out of him are, "Will you come in?"

And the words that come out of her are, "Not today." Which is close enough.

The normal thing, maybe the right thing, to do would be to scream, sharp teeth and growling voice, the kind of language she normally wouldn't let her father hear her use, even at forty-three. But these few weeks apart have changed him. This short exile from her life has washed the color from Heron's face, weakened the way he stands in the doorway even. Maggie doesn't know how to make him hear it, feel it, without him crumbling to dust on the doorstep. Instead, they stand. Maggie outside, Heron in. The narrow porch between them, like the set of a strange play. Heron's coat on the hook, an umbrella leaning against the corner, just in case. Heron tries to explain how hard this is to explain. How at the time it was, or seemed, right and necessary, compulsory even. But he could see that things had changed; he could see how she might see it. She must understand that this was the difficult thing about life. The way things changed, became wrong over time, or revealed themselves to be.

"I'm not blaming other people, Maggie, but at the time, I really thought they were helping me, helping both of us. Things change, don't they? It all changes. It wasn't like now, then." Maggie nods, not in agreement, but to acknowledge something has been confirmed. Put on the record. They stand for a moment, stuck, until Heron moves, breaking away from his position in the hall.

Alone, Maggie leans against the house and hopes the neighbors won't see her, standing on the doorstep, pretending to look at the lock as if she might be fixing it. She thinks of all the energy wasted, the years of hating her mother and mourning her. She wonders if she even has it in her now, the time and strength it will take to reimagine a person she is so used to being without. When Heron appears again at the front door, he hands her a cardboard box full of folders and brown envelopes. Full of her life before.

The unopened birthday cards are the hardest. The earlier ones with badges for five, six, seven, still bulging through the envelopes. The later ones, offering up long-expired record tokens, the unreceived gifts that should have transformed into double-CD compilations or Athena posters. She lines them up on the table, all the unclaimed things.

Maggie separates the newspaper clippings into their own

pile. Heron has kept them loose, which surprises her; they are
calling out for a scrapbook. Articles he has kept, she assumes,
for reassurance, for supporting evidence. She reads all the
headlines, which are about her, and not. Bold print outrage and
moral panic. The breakdown of family values. She observes
how keen they are on cancerous metaphors, on melodrama,
the poor judges and politicians, losing sleep over it all. Lord
Justice Glidewell, smooth, unhindered progress. The name
too good to be true. His words typed on a typewriter, not by
him, she supposes, but a woman in a blouse and well-polished
shoes. One hundred and fifty words of wisdom a minute.

*The ideal environment for the upbringing of a child is
the home of loving, caring, sensible parents, her father
and her mother. When that ideal is unattainable, it is the
court's task to choose the alternative that comes closest
to that ideal.*

Maggie congratulates herself; she is caring. She is sensible.
She is raising her children ideally.

She finds corners of the house where she can think alone. She
takes long baths. One afternoon, she climbs the ladder to the
loft and pretends to sort through the children's old baby clothes
so she can read and reread the pile of documents without anyone looking over her shoulder. She needs time to work out if
this was a thing done to her, or something she is complicit in.
She begins to remember, or thinks she remembers, strangers
with briefcases. Was she offered up as evidence? Stacked up in

the case against her mother, her unbrushed pigtails and sticky hands misread by the court? What easy three-year-old nonsense had she said, or not said, that had condemned them all?

Things come back to her. Memories. In the shower and on the train. Hadn't Heron once told her that, if people asked, she should say that her mother had got a job abroad, or that she had run off with a man she met at the pub. Did she ever say that? To a teacher, or her classmates—did they ask? She tries to hear the rumors that must have been whispered over her head and behind her back. She tries to hear all the words she hasn't heard for forty years.

Her past is not a blank. She remembers plenty about her childhood. The very early part is empty because the very early part always is, that's all. And she really is trying now to remember them, all the people and places she has lost. For the first time in years, Maggie thinks about her grandmother's house, its deep-pile carpets, the shelves of glass paperweights and porcelain thimbles. That house, which was a refuge. And before that, a childhood home for Heron. Washing his freckled face at that sink, walking up those stairs two at a time to bed. Maggie had loved her grandmother, with her houseful of things to dust and treasure, all neatly arranged on mahogany surfaces. She hadn't realized until now that her brain had saved so much of it, a thousand tiny details she didn't know mattered. Fridge magnets sent from second cousins in Australia. Dried flowers on the window ledge. Lemon meringue pie and polishing the brasses. All the comfort, and the safety, of the past.

There are people missing, people missed, but Maggie does

not think she has missed her mother. She had always known not to talk about her, not to bring her up. Any mention of her mother would change the adults around her, a new tone of voice, words that belonged on soap operas, not in real people's kitchens. Maggie remembers that well enough. Her round and chatty grandmother, clouding over each time she said, "Don't mention that woman's name in my house. She's dead to me."

As if it were a matter of personal choice.

As if people could make her mother die or vanish, just by willing it.

Before she goes to bed Maggie checks, as she always does, that the children are in their beds. Asleep. Breathing. She feels, as she always does, the guilt of suspecting she loves them most when they are asleep. You cannot get parenting wrong when they are asleep, she tells herself by way of explanation. That is all it is. Afterward, she sits on the armchair beside the lamp so she can read the pages again, even though she knows much of it by heart already. *It is simple common sense to say that the child ought to have a more normal life in a more normal family.* Words she could recite like terrible poetry. Conor risks a hand on her shoulder. He tries to soothe, to be the voice of reason. He looks through the papers with her again. He reads and he nods and he shakes his head. He repeats Heron's doorstep lines as if they are an explanation.

"I know it's painful, Maggie. But they were different times."

JANUARY 1983

The all-in-one method

Bathtime and her daughter is perfection, the curve of her back, every limb and inch of her.

For a treat, they pour in extra bubbles.

Dawn makes the Matey bottle tip his hat, then they sing, as they always do,

What shall we do with the drunken sailor, as he dances a hornpipe on the taps.

"You'll turn into a prune," she says to Maggie. "Look at those toes."

So she lifts her out and wraps her in a hooded towel.

Maggie asks for icing sugar and Dawn dusts her in talc.

She sits the little girl on her lap and carefully cuts each fingernail, singing their names in turn. Policeman Tall and Ruby Ring and all the rest. Baby Small, where are you?

In the child's bedroom, Dawn reads her daughter's favorite book three times. The cat no more, no less, forgetful each time. "Bother that cat!" they say together, and Maggie begs her to read it again. "Again, Mummy, just one more? Please!" But they have to push on, Dawn says, there are so many other jobs to do at bedtime. Maggie has her own baby to put to bed before she can sleep—her dolly, Julie, who must be tucked into her plastic cot, too. Maggie lays the dolly down softly, its eyes rolling closed, all of its trademark tears dried for the night. Together, Maggie and Dawn tuck her in, her platinum-blond bowl cut resting on the tiny pillow Dawn has made for her from one of her old nighties. All the foreheads are kissed, cold plastic and warm skin, then Dawn stands at the door, promising to leave the landing light on.

In the silence of the house Dawn reads the judgment again. These pages that look as if they have been sent from a fairy-tale castle. The dancing unicorn, a lion wearing a crown.

> *It is widely understood that such women are incapable of natural maternal feelings. It is in the best interests of the child, therefore, that the court awards Mr. Barnes full custody, care, and control of his daughter. Mr. Barnes is likely to marry again. In time the child will find herself, for all the world to know, part of a perfectly normal family. No one need ever know about her mother's deviation.*

The words stick to the inside of her head, the black crust of cooking you have to soak off a pan overnight. Maggie will be better off, they have explained. She will be unashamed.

Heron has given her a few hours to pack. She walks around the house and touches the things she cannot take with her. Things which are too big or not hers anymore. She collects the treasures from the back of her sock drawer. Her flat little

Kodak camera. The tiny plastic bracelet Maggie had worn in the hospital on the day she was born. Dawn folds her clothes neatly into a suitcase. Things she can carry. Her jeans, her favorite cardigan. She has had some of these T-shirts since before she was married. Clothes that have lasted through that life and into this one. Threads and buttons that would outlast them all.

When her bag is packed, Dawn goes into the kitchen. She cracks the eggs into the brown Denby mixing bowl her grandmother gave her for a wedding present. She creams the butter and sugar, she adds the flour. Dawn waits as it bakes, then she watches the cake cool and the night pass. She does not rush, sieving the icing sugar to avoid lumps, spreading one layer of buttercream between the sponges, another on top.

She arranges the chocolate buttons, as she has promised she would, in the shape of the number four. Carefully, Dawn lowers the cake into a tin and puts the four pink birthday candles in beside it. She knows that Heron does not know where the birthday candles are kept.

FEBRUARY 2023

You are still on the fastest route

Maggie isn't completely reckless; she thinks it through, at least the first part. Before she leaves, she makes sure to put something in the slow cooker for later. Not a recipe per se, just vegetables dredged up from the fridge drawer, a tin of tomatoes, enough garlic to make it seem deliberate. She sends six emails and reschedules a meeting. She returns a call. She logs on to Olivia's school website and pays for the trip to Dover Castle. She is efficient. At work. At home. Maggie looks at her life and feels sure that, when it comes down to it, she is a fundamentally good person. She donates to the Lifeboats by direct debit. She almost always buys the *Big Issue*, if she has the right change. Admittedly, she occasionally forgets to feed the cat, but she always resolves to feed him a bit extra the next day to make up for it. She is trying her best. She is coping with all of it, with being a person. She leaves a note for Conor and packs an overnight bag.

The drive eastward is all flatness and farms. Miles of warehouses and pylons, road signs pointing to places that cannot be real, Thickthorn, Hethersett, Cringleford, each sounding more like a pixie village than the last. It's best, Maggie tells

herself, not to overthink the details, what she will do or say
when she gets there. She's not entirely sure yet that she won't
turn around and drive home long before that problem arises.
For now, she is moving forward. She is driving toward her. It
is odd to be alone in the car, the back seat full of the children's
absence. Nobody complaining about her choice of music, no
one to ask, endlessly, how long it will take to get there. Alone
in the car, she has time to think, time to recalibrate. Maggie
has been telling herself the same story for a long time now.
A sad and simple story about who she is. A father, the victim,
abandoned by a wife who didn't look back. A mother who did
not love her enough to stay. This new version is messier, coming together word by word with each page of evidence. The
judge's ruling, the psychiatrist and welfare reports. She hadn't
known things like that really happened, not in her lifetime.
Not in her actual life. But now she does know, and it feels like
reading for the first time. It's one of the few moments from
childhood she remembers so clearly, learning to read. Cracking
the code of letters at five or six years old, the world suddenly
flooding with meaning, road signs, comic books, and the backs
of cereal packets. Words were everywhere, falling into place,
and best of all, they had been there all along, on the fronts of
shops, on the label in her vest. All of that meaning suddenly
visible. Suddenly clear.

When she has tried to talk to Conor about it he says it's a
tragedy, one more sad story in the long list of sad stories we
call history. He feels sorry for everyone involved, of course he
does. Maggie can't name what she feels; *itchy* is the closest to
it. Or *concussed*. She can't stop asking herself if her mother

should have done more? Fought for her more. Stolen her away in the night, as Maggie is sure she would do in the same situation.

"Is that what you would do?" Conor had asked her, and she had shrugged but thought, yes, absolutely. It has always scared her, the strength of this feeling, this truth she has known about herself from the moment they were born. She feels sure there is no limit to the desperate depths she would drop down into for them.

She started the search one evening when the children had gone to bed. Setting up her laptop on the kitchen table because it felt too important for the screen of a phone. Maggie began to type, *Where is my mother*, and Google guessed new endings before she had finished. *She is within*, it offered. Or, *Where is my motherboard located*. She searched social media profiles and small business owners, searching her mother's maiden name, her married name, pulling up faces of Dawns who weren't her. A Dawn Brown who was twenty years too young and married to someone slightly famous. A Dawn Barnes born and raised in Tulsa. The names were too common, or too easily confused by search engines that offered up sunrises over farms and shades of hair dye in place of her mother.

On the second night, she was more honest with the computer, putting all her hope in the little magnifying glass: *How do I find my long-lost mother?* Or more importantly: *Should I look for my long-lost mother?* It was faintly embarrassing, putting all that grief and longing in the same place she searched for cheap flights or a quote on the car insurance. Some questions were too big for the internet. But she wasn't the first to ask. Maggie scrolled and clicked on other people's problems and a memory lurched up to the surface of her thoughts, a long-forgotten day, five years old and lost. She remembers the supermarket shelves, too tall to see over, each long aisle the same, and Heron, nowhere to be seen. Maggie had run and run, searching for him, running finally into the solid middle of a woman, the fat legs of her baby dangling through the shopping cart seat at Maggie's eyeline. A woman who had said, "Don't cry; it's okay. We'll find her. We'll find your mummy."

By the third night Maggie is a sort of missing persons expert, plowing through articles on how to access public records or what to look for when hiring a private detective. She finds companies where you can pay people to do the search for you. She's not sure why this surprises her. Of course there's a market. She watches videos for hours, the success stories, twins separated for thirty years, a great-grandmother found just before her one hundredth birthday, a miracle. The websites are full of people Maggie's age who have never known their parents. They tell the camera they are complete now, fulfilled after all this time, and Maggie clicks on the little cross to make them disappear. There are different websites for the lost causes, people who don't want to be found, or never will be. Maggie reads the stories, sons who had disappeared backpacking, sisters who never came home after a party. Below each blurry photo, the same messages, we just want to know you are safe. We are ready to talk when you are. Maggie hovers around it. The search for a death certificate would be easy enough.

She thinks about contacting the lawyers but finds they have merged with another firm, shredded all the old paper along the way. All the obstacles are a sign, she supposes, or at least an opportunity to let herself off the hook, to say she tried and failed. There is one other name in the court paperwork she has from Heron. No harm, Maggie thinks, in one last search. She worked through the list of Hazel Wrights quickly, before she lost her nerve, filtering out the too young or too old. If they were plausible, she called them, to ask and apologize, to fluster over explanations about who she was and what she wanted. A nurse in Newcastle. A woman who bred Labradors in the suburbs of Swansea. A headteacher smiling out from the About Us page of a primary school website. She googled strangers and asked them if they had known a woman forty years ago, until one of them finally said, "Yes, I knew her. Yes, I know where she lives now. Have you got a pen?"

Maggie stops for a sandwich, the loo. She eats a bag of cheese and onion crisps and thinks about the ways she might introduce herself to her mother. As she drives on, Maggie tries again to imagine Dawn. What she will be like now. What she might have been like then. She cannot remember knowing any gay people when she was a child. Is that true? Only on TV, and then only rarely. For comedy, or the pity of a documentary maker. She remembers the boys at school, something in them that was visible to others, long before they saw it in themselves. The playground insults, she remembers those. When a late bus or a surprise maths test or any other rubbish thing was gay. So gay. Did she say things like that? Didn't they all? She remembers, for the first time in years, the advert on TV with the gravestone that they were all afraid of. And the rumors. You will catch it from a toilet seat. You will catch it from the games mistress if you stay behind after hockey. One of them will inject you with it when you're waiting for the bus.

Having the address changed things, and Maggie saw that she was the one who would have to thaw. That evening, she simply resumed the nightly phone calls with her father, picking up the old habit as if the whole universe hadn't folded in on itself over the past few months. This is how they would fix it, she thought. Not with grand gestures or apologies, but by settling back into his updates about the garden, what passed for gossip about the neighbors. They will get on with it, as families do.

"Would you like to come to lunch on Sunday?" she asked him. "Olivia is practicing for her piano exam, so you'll have to listen to the butchering of 'Merrily We Roll Along,' but if you can face that . . ."

"I'll be there," Heron said.

This is what it would become, something changed but almost the same. Heron would be there on Sunday; he would listen patiently to the plink plunk of the piano. He would find a way of helping Tom with his bike. She will tell him then, whatever there is to tell, about the phone calls and the searching and the drive. She will find out what is at the end of this road, and then she will tell Heron about it.

Now, Maggie points the car forward and watches the clock on the sat nav count down the miles. Her mother's house, three hours and forty-six minutes away from her own in good traffic. The unbearable proximity of it. On the screen, the little blue dot that is Maggie moves closer and closer to the checkered flag that is Dawn's house. In three quarters of a mile, turn left, it tells her. You have reached your destination.

Her legs are stiff from driving and her back clicks when she stretches up and out of the driver's seat. She walks right past the house at first, hardly looking. She will get her bearings. Catch her breath. The village is small, the kind of place you might pass through on your way to somewhere else. Busier, she imagines, in summer. But in February there is nowhere to go, no café to sit in to watch and wait. There is a pub, and a chip shop, not open yet. A little corner shop selling camping gas and lottery tickets. Maggie has come this far; she has looked at the tiny cottage. It is charming, she thinks; that is the word. The flint walls, the front door painted red, a little too small even to convince her that a full-sized person lived inside. She could get back in her car and drive home, or she could knock.

Low water

Inside, the flint cottage is all neatness and faux driftwood signs. The theme is beach clichés, light blue paint, anchor motifs, rope. A sign above the sink reads: LIFE'S BETTER AT THE BEACH. Not untrue, per se, Maggie thinks, but the smugness of people who lived on the coast had always confused her. Still, there is something lovely about it, everything carefully chosen and in its place. The vertical radiators and tidy gray sofas. Every corner of the little house the opposite of her father's, which hadn't been decorated for as long as Maggie could remember, or now she thought of it, since her mother left. Even that seemed completely different to her now. Maggie had always found it vaguely funny, the way her father let the house fade and fall out of fashion. She made fun of it, obviously, and then indulged him as if he were some sort of aesthete, rising above a change in wallpaper on moral grounds. Perhaps she had missed the point entirely. Did he want it that way, a daily reminder of a previous life? A sort of penance? Sadness and disinterest can often look alike, Maggie thinks.

////////

"Shall we walk?" the woman who is her mother asks. "Down to the sea?"

They agree some air is a good idea after the long drive. From the front door of Dawn's house, they cross the narrow main road and turn left, passing the type of pub Maggie is surprised to see still exists, even in a place like this. Happy Hour prices painted on blackboards, umbrellas in the faded colors of cheap Australian lager folded down for winter. Dawn points, indicates they need to turn the corner, and they cut through a caravan park. The not-so-mobile homes are white and lemon yellow, each with the smallest hint of individuality—a Welsh flag, a plastic window box. Clues for a child to follow home. The whole place seems to Maggie as if it is hibernating, closed up and waiting for the warmer weather. In spring, these footpaths would dry up. By summer they'd harden under bare feet and flip-flops, leading people to beach barbecues and salty skin. Here and now, the day is on the turn, the last sharp hour of winter brightness before the evening closes in. They take the steps down, the concrete slipway is too steep, Dawn explains, for her knees.

The walk really is a good idea. Working out where to put their feet keeps them from having to look at each other too much; it stops them from checking for familiar eyes or matching cheekbones. They walk together on cold sand, looking at the sea every few steps, as if confirming it is still there. Maggie does not tell Dawn that she thinks the beach is beautiful; she does not want to be so obvious. She wants, she realizes, to impress her, this woman, with her tidy little house. They start slowly. Like strangers waiting for the same delayed train, they talk about the weather, the general state of things. Both building up to the huge, unsayable topic they have been waiting to broach for years. They hear each other's voices. When they stray into soft, deep grit, Dawn leads them back to the strand line, stepping over wet green stones to the firmer sand. Maggie is glad of her winter boots, writing off the collateral damage to the leather. They can walk more easily now, the sea to their left, the cliffs and caravans to their right. It is another unexpected thing; her mother is a woman who knows about the sea, where to walk, when the tide will turn. She knows the names of all the treasure washed up at their feet. A mermaid's purse, a cuttlefish, the scattered limbs of Gillie crabs.

When they are almost back at the house Dawn says she will cook, unless? The two women, pausing outside the chip shop, swept up in the smell of fried potatoes and vinegar.

"A treat, then. Shall we?"

They carry their parcels of hot paper back to the house, the smell you can already taste. Dawn sets out plates, knives, and forks; she pours two glasses of cold white wine.

The women eat and do not know that they are sharing the same thought, that piping-hot chips after a cold walk is among the best things life can give you.

They both look up at the sound of a key turning in the lock. Dawn is fast to her feet, skipping around the edge of the table to introduce them.

"Maggie, this is Hazel. Hazel—"

"Oh, I know," Maggie says. "We spoke on the phone."

And this, this is a lullaby, too

It is the strangest, most ordinary of evenings. After dinner, Dawn and Hazel fuss over Maggie, telling her to make herself at home over and over. They usher her to the sofa and bring her an extra cushion, as if she will shatter if not handled with care. Maggie sits beside Dawn, a few inches of self-preservation between them. She shows her photos of the children on her phone and Dawn touches the screen, smiles. She breathes through this new agony of learning things she should know already.

Everyone is on their best behavior, the model visitor, the perfect hosts. They try to do justice to it, this monumental occasion. They try to hold back, not to push too hard or go too fast. Maggie studies everything, each inconsequential detail made heavy with meaning. This is the brand of tea my mother prefers, she thinks. That is the way my mother says "chimley," instead of chimney. Everything new. Everything important. Not only Dawn, but Hazel, too. All evening Maggie watches them both, the way they move around each other in the kitchen, the smooth choreography of two people who have lived together for decades. Maggie looks at the photos lined up on the window ledge; they have traveled, seen places, lived. She looks at the precious things they have filled their home with, the framed print above the mantelpiece, the blue glazed bowl where they keep their keys. And she cannot help it, she laughs aloud at the thought.

"What? What's so funny?" Dawn asks, turning from the sink to look at her.

"Nothing. Sorry," Maggie says, trying to pull herself together. "It's just something that popped into my head. *This* was the great scandal the judge saved me from."

"Good job, too," Hazel says. "It's outrageous. Two women in their sixties doing the washing up."

"And in matching slippers," Dawn adds.

Just after half past ten, Maggie starts to consider the practicalities, the drive home too far, the wine too much. There seems very little chance of a hotel anywhere nearby.

"Stay," Dawn says. "You're welcome to. Please. If you want to, I mean. I know it's. Well."

And it is settled.

While sheets are found, the spare bedroom made up, Maggie takes the chance to call home, to put minds at rest. "It's fine," she tells Conor. "Yes, weird, obviously. But fine. Good." She will be home tomorrow. Maggie hangs up the call and sees on the screen a text message from Heron, sent three hours ago, in place of their usual call.

Had MRI scan, very straightforward. Next appointment booked for Monday. Feeling fine. Dad.

Maggie hovers her thumb over the screen. The strangeness of reading her father's words under her mother's roof.

That's good to hear, she types. **Busy tonight. I'll call you tomorrow x.**

And then, just to be clear, a heart emoji.

As she walks back downstairs, Maggie sees Dawn from above, in her house, in her life. She will let this memory overwrite old ones. She will add the details of this night to the growing list of things she knows about her mother. Dawn closes the curtains against the night air, she pours more wine, and as they settle into the sofa, Hazel invents a task she must do upstairs. Nobody is fooled by it, her ruse to make the space she knows they need.

Hazel is barely out of sight before Dawn says it.

"I didn't want to leave you. I need you to understand that."

And Maggie says, before she can think of a way to do otherwise, "But you did. You did leave me."

Maggie feels it like a draft, cold air cutting across them as the words come out of her mouth. She has set it in motion, the difficult questions, the even more difficult answers. Dawn has had this conversation a thousand times before. With herself. With Hazel. With all the various counselors and psychiatrists who have put her back together after the breakdowns that have punctuated her life.

"It was a mistake, doing what I was told," she says. "Thinking I had to. I suppose you know all the details?"

But Maggie doesn't and can't. People, ideas, the country, everything has changed since then, Dawn thinks. It cannot be described, not fully. It cannot be explained, but she tries anyway.

"They told me I was a bad mother," Dawn says, "a dangerous influence." How brittle that seems now. How simple. Maggie doesn't speak, not yet. She tries to listen, to make some sense of it as Dawn tries again to explain.

"The world is full of bad mothers, Maggie. People do terrible things to children. I wasn't one of them. It's hard to think about. What they did to me, to us."

It is physical for Dawn, the retelling is reliving. Damp armpits and water at the back of her throat. Stinging eyes because she will not cry about it tonight. None of it is in the past for Dawn; it is in this room, in her skin.

"But still," Maggie says at last.

"But what? You think I should have done something more? Fought back?"

Dawn is shaking now, worrying the seam of her sleeve. For years she has imagined this moment, practiced what she would say. The words she would use to make it all better for her bewildered little girl. How she would soothe her and make it up to her. But Maggie isn't a little girl, she's a woman, a mother, looking her in the eye and expecting an explanation.

Dawn takes a breath. She presses her hands to her thighs to steady them.

"I asked people to watch you," she says. "The few friends I had left. And I wrote to you, sent things for your birthday. At Christmas." Dawn knows it all sounds feeble now, papery and insufficient. She can't seem to explain how much it took each year to hold the "Happy Birthday Daughter" card in her hand, the impossible small talk at the counter as she paid for it, the moment of letting it drop into the postbox. Each card a little envoy, traveling where she couldn't.

"They said the best thing I could do was leave you alone so you could forget all about me, and I believed them. I believed a lot of things back then that I shouldn't have."

Maggie tries to weigh this. She tries to balance the woman in front of her with the woman she would have been before. A woman of, twenty-what? Twenty-three, maybe? Maggie could hardly keep on top of her overdraft when she was twenty-three. She has to rethink it all. Relearn all the things she has taken for granted as fair and safe and on her side—the law, her father.

Hazel, back with them, leans against the doorframe and sees what they cannot see. Their sameness. This moment, finally here.

"Just tell her all of it," Hazel says, and Dawn tries.

"I did come back. I tried to," Dawn says, "more than once. I asked the solicitors to get me some access. Holidays or weekends, at least. Your dad always said it wasn't the right time. You were settling in at school or had exams. Your nan died. There was always something. And I wasn't always well. Afterward."

Maggie listens, fills in the gaps.

"What I mean is, by the time I was able, they said it was too late, and then, I suppose, it was. All I could do was wait, let you grow up and decide for yourself. I thought you'd find me sooner."

It is all overwhelming, of course it is. It is vertigo and regret and plain cold sadness. Maggie is dizzy with all the new ways to feel angry at the world, and at herself. She feels it then, a kind of homesickness for her life before, and wonders if she has done the right thing coming here. She might have saved them both the heartbreak, just thrown the papers away and carried on. But it is too late, the stone had been lifted, so she says it anyway.

"So. You just got on with your life and forgot about me?"

Dawn swallows. She looks her daughter in the eye and says, "Losing you was the worst thing that happened to me in my whole life, but I was twenty-three, Maggie. What did you think I've been doing, crying in a bedsit for the last forty years?"

For the first time Dawn reaches out to touch her. She strokes Maggie's hair. The gray in it.

"Listen, I didn't go from that to this over a long weekend. When it all happened, I was, let's say, not in a good way. I didn't have a job, any money. My family wouldn't speak to me. Later— I mean years later—I realized the worst thing had already happened to me. When I worked that out, I was invincible."

"I just don't understand how you could have done it," Maggie says again. When what she means to say is, I have missed you. When what she means to say is, I have loved you all this time, even so.

From the other side of the room, Hazel watches them. Maggie, refusing to stand down. Dawn, letting blows land, then drawing the line, protecting herself. It is like watching a mother and daughter fight, Hazel wants to tell them. It is like watching a reunion of strangers.

"I was never going to win custody in that case or anything near it," Dawn says. "But I made a life, Maggie. That is fighting back."

And Maggie finds enough voice left to say, "I didn't get the cards."

It is stupidly late. They have talked for hours; they will talk again. They will piece it back together, try to name what this life has done to them. Maggie knows she is only just beginning to sense the scale of it, the waste. The years it has taken Dawn to become this person with her tidy house and her beachcombing. Although they are both exhausted, neither wants the night to end, so they take it in turns to find ways to say, this is just the start of things. Dawn, who has learned that it is easier to plan than to remember, dares to say, "You could bring the children, when the weather warms up? Are they too big for building sandcastles? I'm not good with children's ages."

"You're never too big for sandcastles," Maggie says, quite certain that Tom would say he absolutely is, and only half sure about where Olivia would stand on the matter. Olivia, at almost nine, one minute posing in front of the mirror, carefully applying her cherry-flavored lip gloss, the next, feeding spoonfuls of invisible food to her dolly. She was in the borderlands now, on the edge of changing into the next version of herself, and Maggie would be there to watch it happen.

Dawn asks to see more photos of these newly minted grandchildren, and Maggie scrolls through the albums on her phone. The children as they are now, taller by the hour, serious. The children they have been over all these years. Squashier and stickier.

"Do you have pictures of you?" Dawn asks. "At this age?"

"At home," Maggie says. "I'll dig them out when you come over."

"There's a woman—two women, I mean—here in the village," Dawn says. "They have a baby. I see them walking together, pushing the pram. Nobody says a word. People smile at them." It had been the work of a lifetime, learning to live with what she had lost. Watching what other people had gained. The fluke of being born at a slightly different time, or in a slightly different place, all that might gift you or cost you.

Maggie takes her mother's hand to hold, the same slim fingers, the same fingernails, the shape of their thumbs exactly alike.

In the spare bedroom overlooking the empty street, Maggie gets ready for bed and reminds herself that she is a finished person. She looks out over rooftops and redbrick chimneys, on a night that is really morning, and thinks of the box file she keeps at home, stuffed with the evidence of her life. Her passport, her degree, her tax returns, all the pieces of paper that prove she is a person. She is a woman with varicose veins beginning in her left calf, a woman who doesn't consistently dye her hair yet but should probably start. She is fine. She has survived this. They all have.

Maggie climbs into the bed and listens to Dawn and Hazel closing up the house for the night. The bolt being pulled across the front door, the dishwasher door thud-clinking closed. She hears them working side by side, doing all the automatic and necessary things that need to be done at the end of even this day of all days. The tidying away and making ready for tomorrow. Waiting for the first moment they will be alone in the darkness of their bedroom, heads dropping back onto pillows, and able at last to say to each other, it happened; it finally came true.

Maggie hears footsteps on the stairs, steady, then pausing at the bedroom door, and she remembers what to do. She remembers how to close her eyes, how to tuck her chin into her chest. Dawn opens the door, no more than an inch, just enough to see, enough to hear the sound of her daughter breathing in. Breathing out.

Author's Note

In the 1980s in the United Kingdom, around 90 percent of lesbian mothers involved in divorce cases like Dawn and Heron's lost legal custody of their children. Exact numbers are almost impossible to trace since most, knowing the likely outcome, chose not to go to court.[1] This novel is not based on a single example, but it does draw on the way real families were treated by the legal system during this period. As Fiona Tasker and Susan Golombok point out, well into the 1990s "it remained the case that many lesbian mothers who went to court were unsuccessful in their quest to keep their children."[2]

One of the hardest aspects of writing this book was the thought that this rift could be imposed on the family when Maggie is so young. When the court case takes place, Maggie is just about to turn four, the age of my youngest daughter when I was writing the novel. While the general legal precedent in custody cases between heterosexual parents was that children

---

1. Rights of Women Lesbian Custody Group, *Lesbian Mothers' Legal Handbook* (Women's Press, 1986).
2. Fiona L. Tasker and Susan Golombok, *Growing Up in a Lesbian Family: Effects on Child Development* (London: The Guilford Press, July 1998).

under six should be placed with their mother, the same rules did not apply to mothers like Dawn. In one judge's report, a speedy removal of a lesbian mother is recommended. "The sooner the change is made the better," the judge declared, describing the four-year-old as "a resilient and adaptable child."[3]

In the rare cases where the continued care of children by lesbian mothers was permitted by the court, the conditions imposed often contravened basic civil rights. Courts might forbid partners from living together, or from showing affection for each other while children were present. Families were often kept under the supervision of the local authority, leaving the threat of being separated hanging over them for years.

The magazine Dawn turns to in search of community and support is inspired by the real magazines *Arena Three* and *Sappho*, the final issue of which was published in 1981. As Steven Dryden explains:

> Access to *Arena Three* was far from easy for many women. Prompted by warnings about the potential legal implications of married women reading the publication, the original founders of *Arena Three* set in place a requirement for married women to obtain written consent from their husbands as part of their subscription requests.[4]

---

3. J. A. Brophy, "Law, State and the Family: The Politics of Child Custody" (PhD Thesis, Sheffield University, 1985).

4. Steven Dryden, "*Arena Three*: Britain's first lesbian magazine," LGBTQ Histories for the British Library, available at https://www.bl.uk/lgbtq-histories /articles/arena-three-britains-first-lesbian-magazine.

While magazines like this could provide lifelines for isolated women, they could also be used in evidence. In the case of *D v. D* (1974) a woman's copies of *Spare Rib* were presented as evidence of her radical feminism and, by extension, her unsuitability as a mother.

The years which pass between the two timelines in this novel are among the most important in the history of the gay rights movement in the UK. In 1988, the Conservative government, led by Prime Minister Margaret Thatcher, brought into law the now infamous Section 28, banning local authorities from teaching "the acceptability of homosexuality as a pretended family relationship."[5] The following decades of restrictions would have had real and painful consequences for teachers like Hazel. Equally, the climate of government-endorsed homophobia would have shaped Maggie's education, and, no doubt, Heron's decision not to be honest with his daughter much sooner.

More hopefully, these decades were also the site of real change. Changes in attitudes and legislation means we leave these characters in a time quite different from the one in which we first find them. The eventual repeal of Section 28 (2003), the introduction of Civil Partnerships (2005), and then equal marriage legislation (2014), as well as legal access to IVF for same-sex couples (2009) has meant that "Parenting possibilities can now feature in the imagined futures of LGBTQ relationships."[6]

---

5. For more, read Paul Baker's excellent guide on the topic: *Outrageous: The Story of Section 28 and Britain's Battle for LGBT Education* (Reaktion, 2022).
6. Jacqui Gabb, "Unsettling Lesbian Motherhood: Critical Reflections over a Generation (1990–2015)," *Sexualities* 21, no. 7 (October 2018): 1002–20.

As I was writing this book I was often overwhelmed by the courage of campaigners and activists who faced what must have seemed an unscalable wall of legal and political pressure. Each of the custody cases I read about was a story of sacrifice and grief. Real mothers and real children. Some of these families recognized that the law would not protect them and so found ways to make the best of private arrangements. Others took their chances, often fighting custody battles over the course of several years. I am a direct recipient of their bravery and their perseverance, and I am grateful.

While the characters in this novel are all works of fiction, the words spoken by the lawyers and judge in the court scenes and repeated in the legal documents are not. Their words are included here as a reminder of how far away the recent past is. And how close.

Acknowledgments

I have many people to thank for making this book possible. I am indebted to my editor, Kara Watson, for guiding me through it all with enthusiasm and admirable curiosity for obscure Briticisms. May your Bags for Life never be sent to the Jumble Sale. Thank you to Nan Graham for amplifying my confidence in this story and for surviving the wettest lunch on record. Joie Asuquo for quick-fire responses and support, Jaya Miceli, Stu Smith, Katie Monaghan, Ashley Gilliam Rose, Rachael DeShano, and all those involved in the design, copyediting, and endless hard work needed to get a book from a writer's desk and into readers' hands. Working with the team at Scribner has been joyful from the first meeting onward.

My heartfelt thanks to Emma Finn and Sarah Fuentes, agents of unwavering good sense and strong nerve.

My final, and biggest, thanks to my family. To my wife, Bethan, for heroic tolerance and early reading. And for my best girls, Orla, Megan, and Wren. I'm sorry there aren't any pictures. You're probably right, those books are usually more fun.